Pra
New Orlear

MW00846902

"I really enjoyed read~~ing this ... it zings along.~~
　　　—James Nolan, author of *Higher Ground* and *You Don't Know Me*

"Rescued By a Kiss is a witty romp through all things New Orleans, from Mardi Gras to king cakes, the French Quarter and beyond. Grab a coffee and spend an afternoon with Brandy Alexander as she encounters a wacky cast of characters found only in New Orleans."
　　　—Sandy Faught, SOLA Member (Southern Louisiana Chapter of Romance Writers of America)

"Colleen Mooney's book is a fast-paced tale set against a backdrop of Mardi Gras madness in New Orleans. The settings sweep from the close-knit Irish Channel to the grace of Uptown and the decadence of the French Quarter. It is obvious that she knows – and loves – the many idiosyncrasies and contradictions of the Crescent City and its inhabitants."
　　—Stephen Rea, Author of, *Finn McCool's Football Club: The Birth, Death and Resurrection of a Pub Soccer Team in the City of the Dead.*

"Mardi Gras in New Orleans provides the backdrop for Colleen Mooney's "Rescued by a Kiss." And what a backdrop it is! Mooney uses the sites and institutions of the Crescent City to full advantage in this raucous romp through romance and mystery. Alexander brings a feisty freshness to her exploits as she rescues dogs and men with equal skill, or is it luck? Her circle of friends includes a rainbow of characters and skill sets and she uses them all in her attempts to solve the mysteries of the handsome stranger: who is he and why was he shot? Can she answer the questions without getting herself killed? Author Mooney kicks off the first volume of her new series, The New Orleans Go Cup Chronicles, with a book containing fun, danger and a lot of canine presence. Terrific!"
　　　　　　　—from The Examiner, Mary Beth Magee-Book Reviewer

"Read the book and loved it. Sort of reminded me of a Grisham novel where the plot is wrapped around local flavor. Even gave a shout out to the 'Jesuits Boys'. Read the first 10 pages of the new chronicle in the back of the book, can't wait for it to be published."
　　　　　　　　　　　　　　—Delta Pilot and Jesuit Graduate

NEW ORLEANS GO CUP CHRONICLES

Rescued by A Kiss
Dead and Breakfast
Drive Thru Murder
Death By Rum Balls

Dead & Breakfast

**Book 2 in
The New Orleans Go Cup Chronicles series**

By Colleen Mooney

Dead & Breakfast Copyright © 2015 by Colleen Mooney
BOOK 2 in The New Orleans Go Cup Chronicles series
Print Edition

ISBN Paperback 978 0 99055 27 2 7
ISBN E Book 978 0 990 5527 3 4

This is a work of fiction. The people, places, and events in *Dead & Breakfast* are entirely fictional. This story is not intended by the author as a reflection of historical or current fact, nor is the story intended as an accurate representation of past or current events. Any resemblance between the characters in this novel and any or all persons living or dead is entirely coincidental.

To My Husband Bill
Thanks for your love and support

Chapter One

"BRANDY, GET OVER here now. There's a dead guy in one of my guest rooms." Julia Richard dropped that bomb on me when she called at 5:55 a.m., and then simply hung up.

I arrived at The Canal Street Guest House at 6:20 a.m. on the humid April morning, let myself in downstairs through the kitchen at the rear of the building—I knew the four-digit code on the back door designed for guests to let themselves in after 11 p.m. when Julia locked the front doors—and headed upstairs.

I found Julia standing over a dead man in one of her guest rooms. She looked like she just stepped out of the shower, and was dressed for the day. One might think this her normal appearance, except for her blood-covered hands. The dead guy was nude, facedown, lying diagonally across an antique four-poster bed. One leg of the bed was broken, causing the bed and body to tilt headfirst at a forty-five degree angle. He had a gash in the back of his skull. Blood was everywhere, all over the sheets and the Oriental rug on the floor. Handprints and fingerprints of blood were on the phone, the bedposts and the dead guy. Looking around the room, I couldn't help but wonder why I would be the first person thought of after witnessing this tableau.

My name is Brandy Alexander and I have lived in New Orleans all my life. My Dad and his rogue brother,

Uncle Andrew, thought of my name while in a bar waiting for me to arrive at Baptist Hospital. The more they drank, the more they convinced themselves that a great New Orleans name for a girl with the last name Alexander would be Brandy. So, just like that, my Dad inked it on the birth certificate before my mother had a say, and she has never missed an opportunity to remind me that I have a stripper's name ever since, like I had something to do with it. My burden in life is a southern, Catholic mother who believes that I am somehow responsible for everything that goes wrong in the world.

"I can't believe this is happening on the first day I'm open," Julia whined when I walked in.

"I can't believe it's happening at all. Have you called the police or just me?" My stomach was knotting up as I mentally indexed things I touched in the mansion during recent visits here to help Julia.

"No, Brandy, do not call the police," she said without taking her eyes off the dead guy.

"Who do you want to call? It's a dead body. What do you think you can do with it? Sneak it over the fence into the cemetery next door? You have to call the police." I froze in mid-reach for the phone in the room when I again saw that it was covered in bloody fingerprints. "Is this the phone you used to call me?"

"Yes," she stood in front of it blocking me from picking it up.

"You didn't kill him, did you?" I started to rub my temples with my index fingers hoping to jumpstart my thinking power.

"No. I don't think so."

"You don't think so? What do you mean?"

"I don't remember much of last night after we got into this room. He opened a bottle of wine he had brought with him and poured us each a glass. I remember I started feeling frisky, then it's all a blur."

"Julia, how much of the wine did you drink? Maybe he slipped you something. Where are the glasses and the bottle?"

"Well, the bottle and the glasses were over there on that tray table or maybe on the dresser, I think. I don't remember how much of it I drank."

"Where are they now? Did you bring them downstairs?" I asked, looking around. The bottle and the glasses were not in the room.

"No. I don't remember moving them." Julia's eyes never left the dead guy.

"Where is the wine bottle?" I asked her again.

"I don't know. I really didn't want any more to drink but he insisted saying it was a fantastic bottle a friend had given him. I don't remember much after a few sips of that wine. Oh, God, this is going to ruin my business." Julia looked deflated. Her normal perfect posture was transformed as her head and shoulders slumped forward like an old woman.

"If you don't call the police, this is going to ruin your life, along with mine. I'm not going to be an accessory to murder. Don't touch anything else. I'm guessing these are all your fingerprints in his blood or did you find some here and decided to add yours to the collection?" I asked, still looking around the room. It was as if the room had been ransacked; bedding pulled off at the corners, pillows everywhere, and a suitcase sitting on the luggage rack, its contents spilling onto the floor. Clothes were strewn from one end of the room to the other, a man's clothes-shirt, pants, underwear, shoes-along with a pair of woman's black stockings and a black lace garter belt. A worn hard shell guitar case was covered in band decals for a group that played throughout the south called The Levee Men and one "See Rock City" decal. It was unopened on the floor and sat next to the suitcase.

The floor-to-ceiling windows were all the way open and the lace curtains billowed out to the veranda. The windows opened high enough so that I could have ducked my head and walked out onto the balcony. Someone shorter than my 5'8" height could walk in and out like a doorway. I could see the sheer curtains waving around the bistro table and two chairs set up out there. An enormous oak tree covered the entire front of the house and most of the porch, making it feel like you were sitting in a tree house.

"The ones in the blood are mine." Julia's words brought my attention back inside. Her eyes were fixed on the body as she spoke to me, "My fingerprints are going to be all over this room. I did the cleaning before this guy checked in."

"How is it you have blood all over your hands? Is it yours or his?" I asked cautiously.

"I thought he was still alive when I found him. I shook him to try to wake him."

"You moved the body?" The police were going to love this fact.

"Yes, but I put him back exactly like I found him."

"Oh boy, with his blood on you, this looks like you did it," I let slip before I realized the effect it would have on her. She went pale and looked at her hands covered in blood as if she just noticed it. "Did you hear or see anything?"

"Uh, uh." Julia struggled with an answer.

"It looks like he put up a fight from the condition this room is in. Did you fight this guy off? That bed is going to need serious restoration." I said, looking at the forty-five degree lean of the antique bedframe. My eyes scanned the room again and stopped on the black lace thong hanging from the chandelier. "Yours?"

"Yes, I guess they are," Julia answered and went pale.

"You guess they are? Was there a third person in your party?" I crossed my arms and shifted into a more comfortable stance. "Go on."

"We, uh, were having a good time, uh, and then, uh, the last thing I sort of remember was the bed broke. We just continued with the uh, sex, uh, until, uh," she trailed off, completely out of "uhs." Her voice quivered, then her body buckled at the knees causing her shoulders, neck and head to roll. She looked like she was doing a full body impression of the wave that goes around a stadium at a football game. I caught her by the arm to steady her.

I wasn't going to get any information from her if she kept staring at the guy. I ushered her out of the room.

"I'm guessing the blood rushing to his head is not what killed him."

"Maybe I did kill him and I just don't remember. I can't remember much of anything after we got in bed. I mean, I remember getting frisky, then the bed broke but everything sort of goes black from there. I know we were getting friendly, but I'm not sure we actually did it."

"Don't ever say that again, the part where you think you might have killed him, not the part where you're not sure you did it. Well, don't say that either. If you killed him, and I don't think you did, I know you would remember. Do you think you were drugged?

"I don't know," she whispered as if she couldn't find the energy to talk.

"We had better go to the kitchen and call the police. Then I want you to tell me everything you remember from the moment this guy checked in. The police are going to ask you, so it would be good for you to start remembering. I'll stay with you and help you anyway I can." This was a cluster if I ever saw one.

Julia had opened a hospitality business in New Orleans. She knew nothing about guest houses or how to manage a hotel and of all places to buy, she chose a former funeral home and crematory on Canal Street. Canal Street, the city's widest boulevard, runs across the entire city of New Orleans, from the Mississippi River to Lake Pontchartrain. The streetcar line makes a stop steps away from Julia's front door. This Victorian, was built in the late 1800s as a private residence, rivaled many of the city's grand mansions, and later was turned into a funeral home since it was located at the edge of the city limits where people came to bury their loved ones. Now, it is surrounded by cemeteries on two sides, around the corner and across the street. It has a columned portico for its entrance and a Porte cochere. The Porte cochere was formerly the side entrance used to allow horse drawn carriages arriving with passengers. When the building had served as a funeral home this entrance was used to accommodate the coroner's van dropping off or hearses picking up the dearly, or not so dearly, departed on their very short ride to their final resting place, next door.

Julia's guest house now used this side entrance to shelter guests from rain as they arrived or departed in limousines or taxis.

Julia had been trying to divorce her husband S.J., but they were at a standoff on who was going to pay for the legal fees. This ended when he suddenly died leaving Julia a widow rather than a divorcee. After his death, she'd found suitcases of money he had hidden at a storage facility, presumably trying to keep it out of the divorce settlement. Now it was legally hers. Today, thanks to that money, she was opening the doors at the renovated guest house and this guy had the audacity to die in one of her rooms.

We went downstairs to the kitchen at the rear of the building where I had earlier let myself in. Julia went to the sink and washed the blood off her hands.

The kitchen was a large room and all the appliances were top of the line. Everything was commercial size, a Subzero refrigerator and freezer, a Viking stove, two sets of triple sinks along miles of countertops with enough Carrera marble to rebuild Italy. Julia had done a brilliant job renovating the abandoned mansion, adding modern conveniences along with beautiful, comfortable antiques. The woman had great taste and after finding the cash S.J. had been holding out on her, she had enough money to buy the best. I told Julia to thank God every day her divorce was never finalized.

"The longer we wait to call the police the worse this will get." I went to the phone on the wall and dialed 9-1-1. I told them the name of the guest house, the address and that there was a dead guy here in one of the guest rooms.

The dispatcher asked if there was anyone hurt or in need of an ambulance.

"Does dead count as hurt?" I asked.

After she paused long enough to convey annoyance or indifference—I mean we are talking about a New Orleans city worker—she said, "That's a no for an ambulance, then. Don't let anyone leave. A police car will be there…shortly." I realized she hung up when I heard the dial tone.

"Start at the beginning and don't leave anything out, but make it quick, the police will be here shortly." I did the finger quotes around shortly but Julia wasn't in the right frame of mind to appreciate sarcasm. "Is anyone else in the building? Other guests, housekeepers, workers?"

"No, no, just him. He told me he came here to play at the Jazz Festival this weekend. He arrived a day early to see some of his favorite New Orleans places before the rest of his band gets in town. Oh God, some of the band members coming in from out of town are suppose to check in later today. What am I going to tell them?"

"Let's worry about what you are going to tell the police. So, how did you end up in his room?"

"After he checked in, he asked me to call him a cab to go to the French Quarter. Oh God!" Julia started wringing her hands.

"What?"

"I took him to the Napoleon House where my friend Andy is a bartender. He was working last night and will remember us having drinks till about midnight."

"Sit down. Take a breath and just tell me everything you know or remember from the beginning. Start with his name."

Julia sat staring at the wall across from her seat at the kitchen island. I went about finding coffee and putting on a pot. After I prodded Julia a few times to stay calm, collect her thoughts and start at the beginning, she finally looked at me.

When the automatic coffee maker made the swooshing hiss with the three beeps alerting caffeine-addicted individuals, such as myself, that it was ready I poured us each a cup. I found a bottle of Jameson's in the cabinet hidden behind a pound of Café du Monde coffee and chicory, powdered creamer, and a box of sugar free packets—Julia's private stash. I added a generous splash of the whiskey to her coffee to help take the edge off her nerves. I was tempted to give myself a splash but it was still a little early and it was a work day for me, even though it didn't look like I'd be getting much done today.

"His name is Guitarzan."

"This is no time for jokes."

"No, he said his friends in the band called him Guitarzan."

"Is he in the jungle band with Jane and the Monkey?" I asked, trying to make her laugh and lighten the situation at hand. Julia ignored me.

"I have been working non-stop on this place getting it ready to open and I needed a break. After he checked in, he came back downstairs and asked me to call him a cab. He wanted to go to the French Quarter. Then he asked if I'd like to go with him and have a drink, so I said yes." Julia's voice was getting shaky again.

"What's his real name, Julia?" I asked, starting at square one.

"Oh, yeah, his real name is Gervais St. Germain."

"Okay."

"Guitarzan" was making sense now. "Where did y'all go?"

"I called a cab and we took it to the Napoleon House, like I said. After our drinks, we walked around Jackson Square and I called another cab to bring us back here. I'm guessing we got back here around 1:00 to 1:30 a.m."

"So, there are two cab drivers out there who saw you with him last night," I said.

She burst into tears. Through tears and sniffles, she rendered the rest of the evening for me. They'd returned and had a nightcap in the salon. Julia went to his room, to make sure he had enough towels. *Who was she kidding?* Anyway, one thing led to another and after a night of whoopee she woke up with a killer headache.

"I realized the bed was broken and figured we'd had a real fun night of it. I felt so bad when I woke up, way worse than I should have felt for only having a couple of drinks. I slipped out the bed so I wouldn't wake him and left his room. I went to shower to help wake myself up. I was in the shower a while and still felt like I couldn't wake up. After my shower I went downstairs to make him breakfast and prep food for the other guests arriving later that day. When I brought the tray up to his room...I found him...like that. I didn't know, I didn't see him like that when I sneaked out of his room earlier. It was still dark."

She told me she'd dropped the tray of food when she saw all the blood. It was still there, all over the floor, just inside the door.

"That must have been a wild night if you two broke the bed," I said.

"Yeah, I guess so, even though I don't remember much after we got into this room," Julia said.

"So, what did y'all talk about last night? Did he have friends here or was he supposed to meet someone else here, since he came in a day early?" I asked her.

"I don't know," she blubbered.

"Anything else? Can you remember anything else about him?"

"He wore a purple stone, I think was an amethyst, on a black leather cord like a necklace. I didn't see it on him when I found him this morning and I know he had it on last night when we went out. He said he never took it off."

"Did he get any messages? Check and see if anyone called looking for him."

We went into the hallway where the answering machine sat on a leggy, gold leafed antique reception desk. It was blinking and indicated there were new messages. We hit play and the first one was a woman's voice saying she knew Gervais St. Germain was checking in. She didn't leave a name but left her number and said, "tell him to call me." The second caller was a hang up and left no message, but the caller did breathe heavily into the phone for a few seconds.

"That's the same weirdo who has called here several times and always just hangs up. It's always from a blocked number," Julia said after she replayed the messages and wrote down the phone number from the first on a scrap of paper on the desk.

I looked at my watch.

"Where are the police?" she asked. Almost thirty minutes had passed since I phoned.

"You should offer coffee and donuts for all cops in this precinct as part of your marketing. Then, they will keep an eye on the place," I said. "Or they might show up faster if you call in for help."

"Now you tell me."

Y Y Y

I LOVE KING Cakes and I don't need to be stressed to eat a whole one by myself, although I would have used that as an excuse this morning. My stomach was doing flips while we waited and I tried to get more information out of Julia. I didn't relish seeing whoever showed up from the New Orleans Police Department. I was bound to know him or her since my ex boyfriend was a cop. I couldn't stop craving king cake.

King Cakes are braided cinnamon rolls shaped into an oval covered in purple, green and gold sugared icing—the colors of Mardi Gras. Someone kicks off the season which starts with the Catholic holy day, The Feast of the Epiphany, giving a party with a King Cake. Everyone at the party gets a piece. There is a plastic doll hidden inside and the person who gets the piece with the doll has the obligation to give the next party the following week. The person who gets that hidden doll gives the next party and so on until Fat Tuesday, the day Mardi Gras is over. These cakes can only be found in New Orleans bakeries during the weeks of Mardi Gras season, or until Ash Wednesday, the day Lent starts. They are the energy food that fuels parade goers. The sugar alone gives you enough energy to maintain the grueling pace needed for weeks dedicated to parading, partying and drinking. It is my official food of Carnival. I could have used a piece right now to help me cope with this mess with Julia. Available everywhere during Mardi Gras, one or two bakeries ship them year round, so I can special order one any time my stress-o-meter screams for some of that sugary saboteur to my normally healthy diet. I was thinking about calling to order one.

Two cups of coffee later, another splash of Jameson for Julia, and my craving for King Cake totally unsatisfied, we still waited. It had been over an hour since I called the police.

While we waited, Julia and I discussed more of what had happened and how much she didn't know about the man who was now dead in her guest room. I told her that when the police arrived she should tell the truth, as much as she could remember, and if she didn't know something, say she didn't know it. If, for any reason, they decided to take her in for questioning, I told her to tell them she wanted a lawyer and not to say another thing. I knew her calling me before she called the police was going to be a problem, but I didn't think it would be a big problem until an unmarked police car, in typical fashion—long after the immediate crises was over— screamed up to the front of the building, lights flashing and brakes screeching as it slammed to a stop. A Ford Crown Vic, the police department's unmarked car of choice arrived, flashed the blue dashboard light and pinched off a single bloop on the siren by way of announcing themselves. The tinted windows didn't allow me to see who was inside. No one got out immediately in spite of their arrival at breakneck speed. When the driver and passenger doors finally opened, a male and female officer got out of the car. I knew this was not going to go well. Julia's chances would have been fine had the first cop on the scene not been my childhood sweetheart and ex-boyfriend, Dante Deedler.

Dante and his new partner.

During the initial aftermath of our breakup, I thought—or was led to believe—that Dante was gay, and that was why our relationship was going nowhere. Local gossip from the old neighborhood where we grew up next door to each other was happy to update me on this recent development...the new partner was also his new girlfriend.

Chapter Two

JULIA AND I walked out to the front porch to meet the police. Dante strode up the steps and introduced himself as Detective Deedler, as if we didn't know him. His previous partner, Joe, had been arrested and was awaiting trial for his involvement in the oil lease scam I'd stumbled into after I kissed the guy I was now dating in a Mardi Gras parade a couple of months ago. Dante and I had not spoken since.

Dante's partner stuck her arm straight out, like a karate punch, holding her shield in my face. I had to lean my head back to read it. It said Z. Hanky. Z stood for Zide, or so the twenty-four-hour satellite operated, neighborhood rumor mill detected and texted me within seconds of obtaining the info. In the past, I would have had to wait for a call over a secure line or a face-to-face meeting at a predetermined locale, like my favorite bar on St. Charles Avenue. The busybody hotline also passed along the useless but interesting tidbit that Dante's police unit had given her a nickname. My face was fighting the urge to burst out laughing at the thought of the other cops calling her Hanky Panky. Dante appeared to be in an ill humor.

"What happened?" he asked, opening his notebook without looking at either of us.

I looked at Julia. She was standing there as if in a trance.

"Julia?" Dante asked not looking up from the notebook. His partner put one hand on her gun, the other on her nightstick and stared at me. I guess I didn't need to introduce myself.

Julia turned around, walked inside and started up the steps. I waited for Dante and Officer Friendly to follow. Dante looked up and gave me an after-you gesture. Detective Hanky followed me with Dante bringing up the rear. We all trudged up the stairs to the second floor guest room. I thought the dead guy looked more ghostlike now. I'm sure rigor was setting in.

This was the first time I had seen Dante in a couple of months. During Mardi Gras a couple of months ago I was told by the bartender of a popular gay club in the French Quarter that he saw Dante in there often, in plain clothes. I thought I had it on good authority that Dante was gay. Turns out, Dante was undercover so I had bad information on him being homosexual. The good information someone shared was that he was pretty ticked off at me for thinking this. Afterwards, Dante and I mutually agreed it would be best if we dated other people. By mutually agreed, I mean, I decided to date other people and Dante ignored me and just went about his business as usual. It didn't help that we'd both lived with our parents right next door to each other since birth, and I was going to be under the magnifying glass every time I had a date. Someone was always ready to report to one of us about the goings on of the other. So, I moved out of the family home and rented half of a shotgun double with Suzanne, another childhood friend from the neighborhood. Suzanne did know when to keep her mouth shut and stayed clear of the gossip rodeo. Over the last couple of months, life had become a roller coaster of adjustments. Seeing Dante for the first time since the move and breakup was harder than I thought it would be, especially seeing him with his new girlfriend at a murder scene.

Julia took a small step over the threshold into the room and immediately moved along the wall plastering herself against it. She stood staring at the body.

Dante's partner leaned over the body to check for a pulse. She looked back at him and shook her head. That's when I noticed her extra wide backside. From the rear she looked as wide as she was tall and I'm not counting the holster with all their police stuff—gun, flashlight, handcuffs, radio—just her big butt filling out a pair of ill-fitting polyester uniform pants. I was feeling tall and thin, and stood up a little straighter.

"Julia, how do you know the victim?" Dante asked her, walking around the room making notes of the havoc, the food on the floor, the disarranged furniture, the man's clothes and the lady things.

"I. He. He's a guest," she mumbled.

"Did you get a name and address when he checked in?"

"His name is Gervais St. Germain and he said he's from here but travels a lot with the band he plays with, The Levee Men. He doesn't keep an apartment here anymore," she answered.

Oh good, I had hoped she would leave off the 'Guitarzan' part.

"Do you know if he has any aliases, nicknames, something else he could have been known by?" Dante asked.

Here goes.

"He told me the band guys called him Guitarzan."

"So are you the gymnast or was Guitarzan here swinging from the chandelier?" asked Detective Hanky, nodding toward the ceiling.

No wonder Dante liked her. She was a riot.

"When did you last see him?" Dante looked directly at Julia when he asked.

"Maybe 5:00 or 5:15 this morning when I woke up and went down to get us some juice and rolls," Julia said. This got a raised eyebrow from the partner-girlfriend wearing, men's polyester uniform pants.

"What is your relationship with this man?" Dante was doing the interrogation while big butt was looking through the dead guy's suitcase for a wallet or an I.D.

"I don't have a relationship with him. He, he just checked in last night."

"How is it you last saw him at 5:15 this morning?" he asked, looking right at the chandelier with the lace thong hanging from it.

"How do you think?" I answered, trying to save her some embarrassment.

"I need Julia to answer the questions, unless of course," he said, pausing and giving me a steely look, "you were here, too."

I gave him one of the stares I'd inherited from my mother and he turned his attentions back to Julia.

"I slept in here with him," Julia stated as if it took her last breath. She looked unstable on her feet.

"Who else is registered here as a guest? We'll need a list of their names along with all your staff, and anyone that comes and goes." Dante cast a sideways look in my direction.

"The registered guests are arriving later today," Julia

said.

"Where are they?" asked Hanky.

"What part of 'arriving later today' makes you think we know where they are now?" I was immediately sorry I'd mouthed off and air fingered the quotes.

Dante looked like he was going to explode, so he busied himself walking around the room taking notes. He stopped and looked at the bloody phone and the bloody handprints on the body. He looked at Julia and asked, "Are these yours?"

She nodded.

"Julia Richard you need to come with us for questioning," Hanky said, taking Julia by the arm. Julia pushed her hands off her. Hanky immediately cuffed her and started to escort Julia out of the room.

"Is she under arrest?" I asked. Hanky ignored me and Dante was calling in a homicide over the police radio, asking forensics to come to the address to meet Officer Hanky. "I think Julia should consult with an attorney before she answers any questions." To Julia, I added, "I'll call Stan and see if he can meet you." Stan was an old mutual friend and attorney. Dante and I had grown up with him.

I followed behind Hanky with Julia and in front of Dante as we walked down the magnificent stairway Julia had spent a fortune to renovate. The width of the grand old Victorian staircase allowed for Hanky to walk side by side with Julia. We stopped at the front leaded glass doors under the fan window.

"You need to come with us, too," Dante said without looking at me.

"Really, Dante? Are we under arrest? What am I

under arrest for?" I really didn't want to be left alone with Detective Wide Side, so being arrested had some appeal.

Hanky never let go of Julia the entire way down the brick entry steps as they left the guest house. "We'll let you know after you answer a few questions." Dante put his hand on Julia's head and guided her into the back seat of the police car.

"Dante, please, can you drive me and my car to the station?" I was right in his face when he stood up closing the door to the squad car. I sounded pitiful whining the question.

He paused and told Detective Hanky to drive the squad car with Julia while he waited for forensics. Then he said he would drive my car and me to the precinct. I thought I saw Hanky Panky going for her gun to shoot me on the spot, but Dante stepped between us and spun me around. He pushed me ahead of him back up the steps into the bed and breakfast.

Chapter Three

DANTE FOLLOWED ME back inside the Canal Street Guest House and told me not to touch anything. The strong smell of the coffee I'd brewed still hung in the air. It was a strong coffee and chicory blend like Dante's mother always brewed early in the morning for her husband and boys before they left for work or school. She would set it up the night before and put it on a timer so it would be ready for them when they got up. Dante was always the first one up. The aroma would drift from her kitchen across the narrow alley between our houses right into my bedroom. It was better than an alarm clock. I closed my eyes thinking of those mornings. Dante would pour us each a steaming cup and come over to sit with me on my front porch. He did this every morning before work and before anyone else was stirring in either house. We would talk about our plans for the day and plan to meet someplace after work. We would meet at either The Columns Hotel to sit out on the veranda or at The Napoleon House, my personal favorite in the French Quarter. We would have a drink and compare what really happened during the day as compared to what we thought would happen over coffee. Mornings were the only time we ever spent truly alone and the smell of the coffee reminded me of how secure I felt talking and sharing my day with him before anyone else was up. I had thought one day after we were married we would sit on our own porch having coffee discussing the three boys I dreamed of having, their little league schedules, having king cake parties and growing old together. We would wake up early and plan who would take the boys to school and who would pick them up, who would get them to their games or dancing school if I had a girl. Dante and I would cook dinner together and we would all eat every day at the same time before he would go off to help our children with their homework. I would press their uniforms and get their lunches ready for the next day. I would put a little surprise in them like a candy or note encouraging them if there was a test or tryouts after school that day. I would make Dante's lunch and tuck a love note in with his sandwich. I would tell my husband how happy I was with him and put a lipstick kiss on it. I would add, 'Be careful and come home to me tonight' on every note. That was what I thought my life would be like.

I wondered what had happened to the happy little kids who grew up next door to each other, played every day at recess and after school. We shared childhood confidences, dreams and secrets. He was my first love, my first kiss, the first boy I danced with and my only boyfriend for most of my life. He was my first love but I guess I was only his childhood friend. Like a good southern, Irish Catholic girl I waited for Dante to bring up our future and marriage. I waited and waited. I guess we didn't share the expectation both families had for us to get married, live on the same block and have a boatload of grandkids for them.

When he left for the military, I waited for him. He didn't ask me to wait, he just kissed me on the cheek and said, "I'll miss you. I'll be back" when I stood with him at the railway station. He probably thought I'd finally move on without him here. I thought he enlisted to get away from me or he would rather be shot at than marry me. He wrote to me but never said he loved me or he missed me. He said he missed home.

He missed home, not me.

I decided to wait for him thinking when he came back we would move on with our lives, together or apart, but, at least I would have an answer. I stayed and lived at home with my parents who happened to be right next door to Dante's parents and four brothers. I had both families keeping an eye on me. We never discussed our feelings for one another, we just heard what our parents said we felt for each other, how we were expected to live our lives together. No one asked us, and we didn't ask each other. He must have hated me for the choreographed life our parents mapped out. I had to wait for him. I had to be right there, in his face when he came back, smothering him along with our parents. Then, to top it all off, when I did kiss someone at a parade, it was right in front of him.

It really didn't endear me to him when I heard, incorrectly, he was gay. Thinking he was gay seemed to explain a lot. Now that he doesn't see me everyday, he can act the way he really feels and I deserve it. He seems happy with his new girlfriend, his new life. I bet he does want to arrest me and lock me up so he won't have to ever look at me again. I wish it had been different when I kissed Jiff at the parade, but I couldn't control how that happened. I wish it had been different so we would at least still be friends.

I waited for him to read me my rights and handcuff me. "Can I sit down?" When I turned around, he was in my face.

"Do what you want." He didn't move.

"So how long have you and Hanky Panky been dating?" I asked trying to lighten the mood and ease the tension I could slice with a knife. However, it came out all wrong. I sounded snippy and catty, like a jealous ex-girlfriend.

"What made you think I was gay?" he asked, deliberately moving closer with each word, causing me to take an equal number of steps backward.

"I don't know. I mean, now I know I had wrong information. I, uh, guess it's because our relationship wasn't physical or romantic. I didn't see it-us-going anywhere." I was being honest. I inched backwards and got a tight feeling in my stomach from him invading my personal space.

"I bought you a ring. I was waiting on you to set a date."

"How was I supposed to know that? You didn't say anything. Dante, our relationship was stuck in neutral. We were more like friends, not lovers. We never talked about getting married. Our parents did."

"I was waiting on you to bring it up." He continued to move into me until my back was up against a wall.

"You were waiting on me to bring it up?" I couldn't believe what I was hearing. "I think that was your job." Then, he was so close to my face I couldn't focus on him, so I closed my eyes.

He grabbed my hands, laced his fingers through mine and pushed my arms up over my head, forcing them against the wall. I wanted to slap him but couldn't free my hands. He stepped into me until his body totally pressed against mine. Our knees were touching. Dante had never handled me like this. The sensation of his body so close and completely all over me stirred both fear and arousal at the same time. His mouth was all over my neck, then my face and when he moved onto my mouth, I kissed him back. Then he let go of me and pushed himself away.

"Is that physical enough for you?" He stormed off to the kitchen.

I stood there waiting for the heat to leave my body. When I regained my composure, I forced myself to think of the issue at hand, which was to help Julia with the problem of the dead guy in the guest room on her first day open for business, and followed him.

Dante was in the kitchen, head down, writing in his notebook. I didn't know how or where to begin. He looked calm, sitting at the table leafing through his notebook until I saw the blood vessel on the side of his face bulging and getting larger by the second. This had always been Dante's tell.

"Dante, I noticed something in that room upstairs when y'all got here and we went back into it."

"You were in that room before we got here?" he asked in total control of his voice, not looking up and writing in his notebook.

"Yes, Julia called me for moral support when she found him. I came right over—"

"What time was that?" he asked, getting back to being Detective Deedler, as though the incident in the hallway never happened.

"I got here at 6:20 a.m. and Julia was so upset that I made the call to the police. I don't know the exact time."

"What time did Julia call you?" He scribbled away keeping pace with the pulsing blood vessel.

"She called me about 5:55 this morning. I drove over here as fast as I could."

"Dispatch logged you in at 6:45 a.m. Why did you wait so long to call?"

"Really? Did you see Julia when you got here? She was in shock."

"Please answer the question."

"Are we going to talk about time and temperature or what happened in the hallway?"

"This is a homicide. Please answer my question." He stopped writing but continued to look at the notebook.

"Okay. As best as I can remember, Julia called me around 5:55 a.m., I finished getting dressed, in a hurry I might add, and came over here right away. I got here about 6:20 a.m. I let myself in the kitchen, walked around looking for her and found her upstairs in the guest room. I asked her what happened and it was hard to get her to say anything standing in the room with the dead guy so we came downstairs. I called the police. Then, I made a pot of coffee to calm her nerves and tried to get her to start talking. And, just so you know, if you had ever kissed me like that, and by that, I mean like you just did in the hall, while we were dating I'd be married to you by now with three kids."

"How did you get in here? Do you have a key or know who else has a key? Don't you think I wanted to kiss you like that? I've always wanted to kiss you like that. Maybe I respected you too much to push that agenda."

He was scribbling again on his paper.

"I know the four-digit code on the back door, so I let myself in through the kitchen. How would I know what you wanted, since we never discussed anything? I wish you would have respected me a little less and kissed me like that a little more." This interrogation was taking a weird direction and I was hoping that not all of it was being written down alongside the murder information.

"So you found Julia standing over the body? Why did we have to discuss anything? You knew how I felt about you."

"Yes, I found her standing over the body. Dante, think about it. Do you really think she would kill him, take a shower, get dressed—*with makeup*—make breakfast, bring it upstairs, drop it all over the floor and not clean it up? You know how compulsive Julia is. Under normal circumstances, she would have cleaned it up and steamed the rug before anyone got here. I wish you had told me every now and then how you felt about me. I would have liked to hear you say it."

"Anything else you remember or that she told you before we got here? I always said you looked nice."

"Well, two things. She did say that he wore some purple stone, an amethyst I think, on a black leather cord around his neck. You know, the short kind that fits snug. He told Julia he never took it off. It was some custom made piece given to him by an old girlfriend. It wasn't on him when I got here. I looked nice? Let's see, 'You look nice' means I love you. How did I miss that?" I bumped the palm of my hand to my forehead. "Yeah, I see how I should have figured out that's what it meant."

"What's the other thing? You said there were two."

"This might not be anything. I wanted to ask Julia but you whisked her away before I could. I remember the front window being open when I first got here. When we went up with you, the curtains blowing in the wind made me realize I wanted to ask Julia if they slept with it open. You know what they say about old flames, where there was fire, there are ashes."

"What does that mean? Are you talking about us?" Dante looked confused.

"It means where there was passion, you know, fire, there will be ashes when the fire's gone. It means there's always something left from a relationship. The longer the fire burns, the more ashes, the more memories. We have a lot of memories. I'm sorry I hurt you. I never wanted to."

There was a knock on the front door. He stood up to go answer and said, "I've been in love with you for twenty-seven years—since the day I first saw you when your parents brought you home from the hospital."

The knock on the front door announced the arrival of the forensics/crime scene people interrupting the only personal conversation Dante and I had ever had regarding our future. It was only 8:15 a.m. and I felt drained. I still had to call an attorney for Julia and get to Central Lockup to bail her out of jail.

Chapter Four

DANTE SAID I could leave the guest house when forensics arrived. He said Hanky would come back for him and they both needed to see what they could find at the crime scene. On the way to Central Lockup on Broad Street, I drove to my office, which was inside the main switching station for all data and voice traffic for one of the biggest telecom companies in the world. After punching in the code to raise the steel door to the parking garage on the first level, I took the elevator. After entering another code so the elevator would deposit me on the correct floor, I ran in, grabbed mail and messages from my office, and advised our assistant I would be working at home and to please forward all calls to my cell phone. I'd been recently promoted from sales to the group that investigates telephone and internet fraud. I still had the same large customers like hotels, shipping companies, and several universities in the state, only now I worked with them on different issues. Unbeknownst to me at the time, the F.B.I. vetted me, and my association with the local police, i.e. Dante, when I applied for the job. All I knew about Dante's tour in the military was that he didn't care to discuss any of it. If I asked him any questions about his whereabouts or jobs while on active duty, our conversation would stop abruptly, or he would walk off and ignore me. I thought this promotion had something to do with my affiliation with Dante, even though I didn't feel comfortable asking anyone to confirm it. Some of Dante's military pals came to visit him and I met them one evening. All of them did the zip the lip move when I inquired about what they did in the service. I decided it was better if I didn't know.

I flipped through my mail and called Stan Fontenot, now an attorney and my friend from childhood who had helped me in the past. The conversation did not go well for Julia.

"I don't take criminal cases."

Stan did take criminal cases, but his history with Julia wasn't favorable and he had made it clear he didn't want to be anywhere near her ever again.

"Criminal? Julia is a felonious pain in the neck, but a criminal? C'mon Stan. I know Julia is a little outspoken. You know I'll be there." Julia needed to work on her people skills and she was often in dire need of a filter before she spoke or thought. Honestly, I think Stan was afraid of her. "If you take it, I'll buy you lunch or dinner at Commander's—your choice."

Stan said, "I'll buy you lunch and dinner every day for the rest of your life at Commander's Palace if you don't ask me to take this case. Brandy, you know I luv ya, but you can't control what comes out of her mouth. Given the circumstances she would be better served by an attorney who has more experience with criminal cases. They know how to avoid the case going any further and by not going any further I mean get a firm who can put this matter to rest before you have to have Julia speak in front of a judge, courtroom or jury."

"Oh, c'mon Stan. I don't think Julia's feeling particularly flippant over this."

Then, Stan suggested I call Jiff Heinkel's office. That was a laugh. My Jiff. Parade kiss Jiff. No more trying to talk Stan into this one.

The Heinkel father and son law firm in New Orleans had a big criminal practice. Jiff and I were working on a relationship since he's the guy I kissed recently at a Mardi Gras parade and the reason I broke up with Dante. I called him, explained what happened this morning and asked if he would represent Julia, or at the very least help me get her out of jail.

"Brandy, are you all right? I'm so sorry you had to see that this morning, someone who'd been murdered. That's tough," Jiff said.

"Yes, I'm fine although I'm exhausted already and it isn't even 9:00 a.m. Can you help her? I need to go bail her out."

He said he would make a few calls and try to get her released by the time I got to Central Lockup to pick her up. I advised him I would be there in an hour after I made a few more calls.

"Don't rush because you may still have to wait when you get there. And, hey, what are you doing for Jazz Fest this week? I'll take off work and we can go Friday. I hate going on the weekend. It gets too crowded," he said. "Plus it might be a bit of fun after all this craziness."

"That sounds great. I'll see if I can play hooky from work too. Call me later." Smiling from ear to ear, I heard the dial tone and sat a minute with the phone still to my ear wishing we had more time to talk. Jiff was the perfect guy. He was accomplished, came from a great New Orleans family, his mother was a judge, his dad had the law practice with Jiff and his brothers. Jiff's sister was in law school waiting to join the family firm. He was a classy guy, great dresser, a lot of fun and was always up for anything I wanted to do. He took me sailing, we went to wonderful parties for the charitable causes he supported. He loved to see me get dressed up and take me out. He also loved dogs, Schnauzers in particular, the breed I volunteered doing rescue work for. The fact that he had one was a bonus in my book.

I made as many phone calls as I could before leaving my office trying to handle work issues before I went to Central Lockup. When Dante had released me to leave in my own car, he had said I was still a person of interest and he knew where I lived if he had more questions. He knew where I used to live, and that was with my parents right next door to him and his parents. I never told him I'd moved into an apartment in Mid City that I shared with Suzanne, but I'm sure some Nosey Nellie Neighbor had. Even if you've never met a person before, you only needed to talk to anyone who grew up here for five minutes to discover that you know someone he or she knows. Everyone knows someone you know in New Orleans. It's the biggest small town in the U.S.

Nothing in New Orleans happened fast, and neither did Julia's release from Parish Prison. New Orleans criminal complex at the corner of South Broad and Tulane Avenue is a plethora of buildings dedicated to every infraction of the law you can imagine, often done by those to those they know and love. Police Headquarters is located here. Even if you didn't know that, it's easy to tell because there are a zillion police cars parked everywhere— illegally. The Criminal Court building is here, Night Court is here, the Municipal Court for minor offenses is

there and see what they plan to do with him."

"Today? You let him outta here today? After he beat on me, you gonna let that good fo' nuttin' go after he been talking with that skank?" The woman became animated, punching the glass in front of the officer's face and screaming so loudly that two deputies flew out from behind a steel door, each grabbing her by an arm and escorting her to the exit commanding her not to return. When she tried to re-enter they stood shoulder to shoulder blocking the doorway. One deputy said, "You come back here and we'll arrest you for throwing hot grits in his face. That's why he's at University Hospital."

University Hospital was now the default public hospital since Katrina devastated Charity to the point it had not reopened and didn't look like it would. The woman left jabbering away something incoherent and waving her arms over her head.

The man in front of me was looking back over his shoulder at the excitement. We made eye contact so I said, "Boy, she must be some jealous type if she got that angry over her man talking to someone."

"Talking is slang for sleeping with that other woman," he answered.

I didn't make any more comments or even eye contact with anyone else for fear of getting into an altercation over the local lingo and provoking the two deputies to reappear and escort me to the exit.

Next up was another situation regarding similar indiscreet communication. The woman stated this was her fifth time at the window and her persistence to learn her husband's exact release time made me wonder why there wasn't a metal detector where we had to walk through to get in here. We all knew he was better off inside the big house because the little woman found out he was fooling around with her sister.

No one was spared or given the slightest shred of discretion. Forty-seven minutes later I stepped up to the glass and asked about Julia's release time. The speaker stuttered that there was no information on Julia Richard at this time and to check back later. Did they think we all had nothing to do but stand—not sit—in this hellhole and wait for another opportunity to get back in line for the same stimulating conversation over the airways?

When it was my turn again, I advised the officer on duty that I was there to pick up Julia Richard or Julia Sawyer. She was back to using her maiden name of Richard. He informed me she was still in booking. To take a break from the redundant nature of Central Lockup's waiting room, I walked across the street to gulp air not laden with disinfectant fumes, and bought a coffee at the Latte Da Coffee House. I took my time drinking it while sitting in the luxury of what looked like a federal reserve café with bars on the windows and enough bullet proof glass across the counter reinforced with wire mesh to stop an assault with an automatic weapon.

Like the waiting room of Central Lockup, this coffee shop had a two-way speaker to place your order through, and then you'd put your money on a Lazy Susan type revolving plate. The plate spun around with the money and at no time did a sliver of an opening from the inside allow infiltration from the outside. After they had your money, you got your order, with any change, on the plate turned back to you. I requested additional napkins and the turn style spun back into action sending out one more paper napkin.

After I got my order, I wiped off a chair to sit and sip my coffee. Unlike Central Lockup, a comforting smell of coffee and baked bread wafted in the air.

I remembered Dante told me once, "Someone, most likely in a bar during happy hour said, eating hot and spicy food in hot climates is supposed to make you feel the heat less." The idea is supposed to force the body to open its pores thereby allowing your internal temperature to equalize with external and fool yourself into thinking you weren't melting. Not me. The coffee had the same effect the kiss from Dante had on me. My internal thermostat felt like it was pushing steamy mercury up my spine from my toes to my head. I sipped the hot coffee, closed my eyes and I was back against that wall in the hallway with Dante pressed all over me. I felt his mouth all over my face and I closed my eyes swallowing the hot liquid, feeling it spiral down, then shoot a heat wave right back up my spine. I was going over every detail of that encounter with him in my mind, adrift in an erotic, sensual moment...when a voice that sounded like the fingernails on a chalkboard kicked me out of my warm and fuzzy state.

"BRANDY ALEXANDER! Why as I live and breathe, is it really you? What are you doing here?" screeched the voice I knew to be my cousin Pootie in that nanosecond before opening my eyes and seeing her round, sweaty face in front of mine. Pootie was my annoying childhood nemesis and goofy cousin. When my eyes popped open I was back in one hundred per cent humidity sweating instead of feeling the glowing heat of my Dante moment.

When we were kids, Pootie got everything she wanted because she was the only child, and adopted. I'm sure my mother believed I was the reason Pootie was an orphan in the first place and she never missed an opportunity to remind my sister and I of it, "Poor Pootie, she's adopted. Be nice to Poor Pootie, share your toys with her...she's adopted. Poor Pootie, give the bigger piece of the candy bar...she's adopted. Poor Pootie, blah, blah, blah, Poor Pootie." The facts were Poor Pootie got to wear a bra first (even though she didn't need it to this very day), Poor Pootie got to drive first, Poor Pootie got her own car first, demanding a brand new convertible, not the second hand clunker I was happy to receive. Poor Pootie got to date first, and on and on. Poor Pootie and her sense of entitlement always made me want to slap her by way of saying hello. My sister felt the same way.

Now, I had let her covertly sneak up on me while I had been distracted in my hot zone. As kids, when our mothers took us all shopping on Canal Street at D. H. Holmes, we were forced to hold hands with Pootie so she wouldn't get lost. No one worried if my sister and I got lost. My sister and I would run away from her and hide inside one of the long winter coats hanging on the wall in the men's department. My mother would have our names called out over the department store loudspeaker as lost children. Some well meaning sales clerk would find us and return us to her.

The second my eyes snapped open I imagined myself saying "No, Pootie, you think you see me. This is your imagination. I'm not really here. Are you on medication?"

Instead, I refrained from an eye roll and kept my face void of all expression as I stood up saying, "Nice to see you, but gotta run. I've got to get back to my office."

"Your office? Where are you working? Is it close to here, maybe we can have lunch? I work right across the street. Wait up, I want to talk to you," Pootie huffed and puffed as she tried to keep up with my giant strides out the door as fast as her short fat legs could propel her, following me down the steps and to my parked car.

I didn't want her to follow me back across the street into Central Lockup asking a million of her mindless questions only to run to the nearest phone to call my mother and tell her where she'd seen me. That was probably going to happen anyway. I didn't want to give her more ammo to use against me, so I walked to where I'd parked my car, got in and locked the door. I looked at her through the driver's side window and tapped my watch with the other hand mouthing the words, 'gotta go.' I waved goodbye, drove around the block and parked in a different lot. You can't be too careful when trying to avoid Pootie. I remembered she worked somewhere in the area either at the police station or a bail bondsman office, so waiting in Central Lockup was not the safest place to avoid seeing anymore of Pootie. I would need to be more covert.

It was late, around 11:00 at night when Julia was finally released. I had been there waiting since 10:00 a.m. A loud buzzer sounded over a Klaxon horn and doors grinding metal against metal could be heard. Then the massive barrier keeping us from them, opened and Julia drifted out.

I grabbed her arm and headed for the door. "My God, Julia, is that you that smells like that?"

"Brandy, this place is a cesspool."

"OK, Julia, let's wait until we're outside."

"You won't believe what it's like in there. I need to find a hose to rinse myself off, I don't want to get in your car like this," she said. I escorted her out as fast as I could.

"What is it? What smells like that?" I made a face trying to keep the smell from invading my nasal cavity. It was worse than the waiting area smell.

"It's me. The inmates in there throw urine or feces on everyone new who comes into the general holding cell."

"Oh, that is rank. What do you mean—they throw urine on you? Why don't the guards stop them?"

"The guards…" her voice sounded tired and defeated, "the guards make a big deal of announcing the new target when they lock up a new guest of the city."

Chapter Five

I STOPPED BY Julia's bed and breakfast after work a couple of days after I sprung her from lockup to find a handyman doing odd jobs at her guest house.

"Who's that?" I nodded toward the front of the house, where a man in overalls was working in the flowerbeds.

"Oh, that's Frank. I met him on the inside during my first, and hopefully last, incarceration. He kept some of the guys from pelting me with urine and feces."

"They put men and women in the same holding cell?" I asked, outraged.

"No, but they might as well have. The cells are on either side of a narrow hallway. They don't reach for you when you pass because the guards will hit their arms outside the bars with their nightsticks. So, they pee at you through the bars."

"So, you hired someone who peed on you? Did someone hit you on the head in there? That would explain why you have suddenly gone out of your mind. What do you know about this guy? He could be dangerous."

"What? No, not Frank. He kept the others away from me. He's a nice guy." Julia was preoccupied looking for something in a drawer.

"Do you know what he was arrested for?" I asked.

"When it was relatively quiet for about five minutes

we chatted. He said he was booked for sexual harassment when he approached a woman, a little too closely according to her. He said he just wanted to admire her broach."

"You could have a sexual predator here, did you think of that?"

"Some drunken tourist made the complaint. She thought he was coming on to her. He's harmless, and hasn't made any untoward advances with me except to admire my jewelry. I could use a handyman and he says he's done all sorts of odd jobs."

"Julia, think. What if he's a thief? He might be casing your guest house." I couldn't believe she would just pick up with someone she just met in prison and hire him as a handyman.

"Miss Julia?" The man we were discussing approached, wearing a gray work jumpsuit with his name, FRANK, written in script with a purple Sharpie above the chest pocket. He was about a head shorter than Julia who stood 5'10 in stocking feet, wore four inch heels and had "big hair" that added at least 6 more inches to her height. In his pocket he carried several colored markers inside a vinyl pocket protector. For a handyman, he sure was tidy about his person and dress. "Excuse me for interrupting you, but I finished hanging the curtain rods and cleaning the flower beds. Is there anything else you need me to do?" he asked.

"I have some towel racks and hooks I'd like you to install in the bathrooms." Julia walked off and returned with a box of items, handed them to Frank and gave him the room numbers where they needed to go.

I stayed and was about to make small talk about the

weather with Frank when he grabbed my hands and asked, "Where do you get your nails done?" He started to scrutinize my manicure before I could say the weather was Africa hot.

"Oh, I've been going to the same manicurist now for awhile. She's in the Fairmont salon where I get my hair done."

"Tell me you don't go to Blaze's Salon!" He all but squealed as he placed both hands on either side of his face. He had long manicured nails for a handyman. "I worked there forever as a shampoo girl, and I love the way that little Asian girl did nails. Then, Blaze promoted me to his assistant."

Shampoo girl? Did I hear him right? Instead I asked, "His assistant? At the salon?" I made a mental note to ask Blaze about him at my next appointment.

"Oh, no, my job was to be his assistant in his antique shop on Magazine Street."

Blaze's salon was upscale, expensive, and catered to the wives of New Orleans' captains of industry. He had a waiting foyer that looked like the hotel lobby where his manservant brought complimentary champagne, gourmet coffee or mineral water (plain or sparkling) to his waiting patrons. He updated the salon regularly with antiques from his shop on Magazine. The grand dames of the Garden District were his clients, both for the hair salon and they would also buy the antiques and collectibles he had on display. There was a never-ending parade of something new being ushered in and out. Then I realized I had seen Blaze directing Frank, dressed as an elf at Christmas, decorating a fourteen-foot tree in the foyer of the salon.

"Yes, I think I do remember you there. Weren't you an elf decorating the tree at the salon?"

"More like a slave elf. Blaze had us moving all that heavy furniture in and out of the shop, which was bad enough, but then he had us deliver it to all those old biddies uptown. They could never make up their mind on where they wanted it so they made me keep moving it around until they decided where they liked it best. All of them lived in two or three story houses and they never moved it around on the same floor. No, it was always, 'Frank, see what it will look like in the bedroom on three,' or 'Frank, move it back down to the first floor in the breakfast room'. I didn't make enough tip money to buy all the Ben Gay I needed every night after furniture deliveries. I asked Blaze for a raise or to go back to being the shampoo girl"—*there, he said it again*—"and he fired me."

I was just about to ask him when he left working at the salon since I had been going to Blaze for at least two years and only remembered seeing him once, in an elf suit around the holidays more than a year ago, when Julia returned with the box of towel rods and instructions on where to hang them. Frank scampered off to finish up the bathrooms.

"Julia, did you notice anything unusual about Frank?" I asked after he went off with his new assignment.

"Like what?"

"Well for starters, I think he's wearing mascara. I just noticed it while you went to get the towel bars," I said. "And his eyebrows look funny, like maybe he plucks them." I was about to add the fact that he said he worked as the shampoo girl where I get my hair done when she cut me off.

"Don't you think I know he's a metrosexual? Don't you think I know a metrosexual if I see one? If I didn't know, I would have guessed soon enough. I've caught him in my private office using my makeup and trying on my clothes. I told him if he touches the Elizabeth Arden face cream that I paid two hundred dollars for I would kill him. If you have something you want to talk to me about, follow me. I need to start the afternoon snacks for the guests."

Julia didn't take kindly when you pointed out anything she overlooked or didn't know. The fact she thought a metrosexual was the new term for transgender wasn't as big a deal as her saying she would kill Frank. That might not bode well given her circumstances with the recent arrest.

I just let it go.

"Yes, I did stop by to see how you were doing, and to tell you I called Stan to see if he could handle your case."

"Stan? Stan hates me."

"I don't think Stan hates you, but his workload is such that he couldn't take the case." Ok, that was a white lie but it's forgivable if you tell it so you don't hurt someone's feelings. "He referred me to Jiff and his dad's firm. I wanted to see if one of the attorneys in his firm made any contact with you to help you with this, this, uh, situation."

"With the arrest. Go on, you can say it. Yes, I did and some investigator is coming by here this evening to get everything I know, I saw, I said, I heard, blah, blah, blah. In fact, you should be here too. He mentioned if anyone else was here at the time of the murder—yes, that's what they are calling it, a murder—then it might be helpful since you might remember something I don't."

"Sure, I'll be here. What time?"

"About 6:30 is when he said he'd drop by. I told him by that time my guests should all be out to dinner or the French Quarter. Excuse me. Frank, please bring us a Sazerac on the veranda."

Ÿ Ÿ Ÿ

SITTING ON THE front porch just outside the floor to ceiling windows of the double parlor, we waited for the investigator. The garden in the front of the house had mature oak trees, their lichen crusted limbs draped with moss reaching for the sky over the roof and shading the house. The fragrance of the sweet olives strategically placed in the front garden of the home kept disgusting street smells of horses and garbage from an earlier time to a minimum inside the home.

Frank appeared with two drinks on a silver tray. He had changed into black palazzo pants and a ruffled tuxedo shirt complete with bow tie. Julia didn't seem to notice the change in his ensemble but when he left, she asked, "Do you think the ruffled tuxedo shirt is too much? Don't you think a pleated one would look better?"

"Well, you have the better eye for putting outfits together, but yes, I think a pleated tux shirt would look more elegant and a lot less like a prom tuxedo from the 1980s disco era," I said. She looked pleased with her decision and went to advise Frank of the wardrobe change. When she returned, we sat and enjoyed the fragrance of the sweet olives with our Sazerac while we waited.

A convertible BMW pulled up and a tall, lanky twenty-something year old guy got out holding a scuffed, brown leather covered notebook. His peach colored rumpled slacks needed a date with an iron, as did the green striped button down shirt, open at the collar that he wore with loafers, no tie and no socks. His full head of wavy blonde hair had a tossed, uncombed surfer dude look. His Yuppie-ness appeared to be fresh out of a Tulane frat house.

"How y'all doing, ladies?" A casual smile sprawled across his baby face when he loped up the steps, to where we waited on the porch swing. His arms and body swung in rhythm opposite his casual stride. He had to lean forward and down a bit to extend his hand to shake Julia's, and then mine. "I'm Ernest Devereaux and I'm here on behalf of the Heinkel Law Firm to ask you some questions. Are you Miz Richard?" He pronounced Julia's name correctly, just drawn out, like Reeeeeeeee charrrrrrrrrrd, so I knew he was a local boy.

"You're the investigator?" Julia's tone questioned not only his title, but also his ability and qualifications. He smiled by way of an answer.

After the handshake I asked, "So, how long have you been working as an investigator?"

His posture straightened and it seemed the wrinkles in his pants disappeared. The languid speech changed and stated with a no-nonsense abruptness. "I usually work undercover around the universities, let's just say monitoring illegal activity, and leave it at that. I've been in law enforcement for fifteen years. Mr. Heinkel asked me to personally handle this one." His answer lost all the southern charm and had a hard edge to let us know he was all business. His demeanor changed with the accent and it looked like someone more formidable appeared in his place.

He was more cop now and showing his true age. It worked for me. He stated we should go inside and he wanted Julia to show him where she'd found the body. Inside there was no sign of Frank, even though he was supposed to be at the reception desk answering the phone.

The guest room still had crime scene tape over the door, which Julia had covered with a curtain on a spring rod across the doorframe.

"Nice touch," Ernest said looking amused.

"Well, I can't have guests thinking this guest house might be their last stop before the cemetery next door," Julia said.

Ernest entered first lifting the crime scene tape with one hand for us to duck under, and pointing with his other for us to stand just inside the doorway.

"Are we allowed past the crime scene tape?" I asked.

"I'm an investigator for the defense," he said pulling out his wallet and flipping it open to show me his credentials. "But not really, so don't touch anything. I want to see if I spot something the crime scene photos missed." He walked around the room, asking questions, and I busied myself looking out the window. I realized the big oak's massive limbs totally hid the wrap around veranda from the street, including the two front windows and the side window overlooking the cemetery next door. Anyone who was just a tad bit nimble could have climbed the tree to take a look into the room, walked out on the good sized limb closest to the handrail and stepped onto the porch. That person could have left the same way. No one would see him from the street and no one in the cemetery next door was going to leap from a grave to call in a 9-1-1.

"Ernest, I told the police I remembered the window being open when I got here and found Julia in this room. It was open when we came up with the police."

"I keep the windows closed and locked. I can't remember if Gervais opened it when we were in here or if it was even open when I left in the morning. I was pretty out of it. I had a monster hangover even though I'd only had a couple of glasses of wine," Julia said.

"Maybe someone came in that way," I said.

"It looks like the police dusted for prints. I'll see if I can get their report," Ernest said to no one in particular while he snapped a bunch of photos with the cell phone he pulled out of his shirt pocket. Julia and I looked at each other and shrugged.

"Julia was hauled off to the pokey, and I was detained downstairs and questioned. I was released from here when the crime team showed up. I stopped at my office to pick up messages and say I'd be out the rest of the day, and then I went to Central Lockup to get Julia out where I waited until 11:00 p.m.," I said.

"Well, I'm sure your prints will be everywhere since you own the place. Who works for you cleaning or doing turn downs?" Ernest asked Julia.

"It's only me here now. Frank came to work here after the incident but no one has been in here except the police, me and..." her voice trailed off. Ernest and I didn't make her say his name. I was afraid she would call him Guitarzan again.

"Oh, Julia, tell him about the phone calls before the guy checked in and after," I said.

"Right. There was one call that was date and time stamped the same night Gervais checked in. He asked me out for drinks. That call came in while we were out. After that one, there were a couple of messages with only heavy breathing. All the other calls left messages or were about making reservations. There were no more weird calls after, after…" Julia drifted off.

"Who was the caller? Do you still have that? Did you give it to the police?" asked Ernest.

"It was a woman's voice and she asked if Gervais St. Germain was a guest, waited for someone to pick up and then said she'd call back. It was like she didn't know she was speaking to an answering machine. I think she left a number but I don't remember where I put it," Julia said. Then we all headed downstairs to the hall where my big deal with Dante happened. Frank was nowhere to be found. I thought he might have left for the day without advising of his departure.

We searched and there was no piece of paper with a number and the message machine had been erased. Ernest asked if Julia might remember the name. Julia said she didn't leave a name only the number.

The detective gave us each his card and said if she did remember or thought of anything else, to call him.

As soon as he got into the BMW to drive away Julia said, "I'm screwed. Why didn't I keep a copy of that number from the caller ID?"

"Why did you erase it?" I asked.

Chapter Six

I KNOCKED ONCE and opened the unlocked front door of my parents' house. It seemed like I was walking into a burglary or a stick up. Everyone was screaming because our Italian neighbors were visiting. I was about to back out quietly so I wouldn't be noticed when my dad spotted me.

"Well, look what the cat dragged in!" His rosy cheeks gave off the same hue as the red wine he was sloshing around in his glass. "C'mon in, we're celebrating Little Angela getting married to Angelo Tuddo." My dad loved any excuse to celebrate, since living with my mother, a teetotaler, paid his penance forward in life.

The Fortunatas, Angelo Tuddo and my family were all there. Little Tony, Little Angela's twin brother was named after Big Tony, their Grandfather. Angela's parents were Mr. Donnato and Miss Angela Fortunata. My dad grew up with Donnato at his house listening to Louis Prima's music. Good New Orleans manners allow children to address adults they know or are familiar with as Mr. and Mrs. First Name. We use Mr. and Mrs. Last Name, even as adults, to address strangers or people older than us unless instructed otherwise and that still feels awkward.

Mr. Donnato would say, "Your dad was the only mick in a room full of us dagos right off the boat. He called my dad 'mick' so much a lot of people thought it was his name. Mr. Donnato called me Little Mickey when I went to their house to play after school. He said I looked more like my dad than my mother and I should have been named after him. I liked Mr. Donnato.

Little Tony grabbed me before I could out maneuver him, giving me an all too friendly kiss on the lips. He was squeezing my shoulders so tightly my ears could almost touch them. "Can you believe my hook-nose sister got some dago to marry her?" he yelled with my ear too close to his face. The entire family needed to practice volume control.

"Oh, my God, don't talk stupid, Little To-o-o-ny. How many times I gotta tell you, she has the big nose but, thank God, it doesn't have a hook in it." Miss Angela stood up wringing her hands, and crossing herself every time she said 'God' which sounded like 'Gawd' while reprimanding Little Tony. She crossed herself a lot when talking because she said 'God' a lot. She had the same speech pattern as Little Angela. I looked at Little Angela, wondering if she had gone deaf and then I realized she was on her best behavior in front of her fiancé. She could very well hear everyone and take up for herself since we were all in the same room and she had given Little Tony a black eye or two when we were kids for a lot less.

"Hook nose," he called Little Angela again after his mother sat back down. He continued talking to me, holding his hand on one side of his mouth as if this broadcast was meant for my ears only and the rest of the room was not tuned in. "Yeah, so anyway, Angela hooked a whale, in all senses of the word, to marry her soon to be knocked up ass."

"Dat's enough." Mr. Donnato, Little Tony's dad, put

down his glass of wine and started to hoist his largeness off one of my mother's dining room chairs screaming under his weight. Little Tony got the message, let me go, and scampered to stand behind his mother.

"You remember Little Angela, right Brandy?" my mother asked. How could I not remember her, or this circus scene I'd seen every time I went to play at her house after school. We went to the same grade school every day on the same school bus and sat next to each other every grade until we left to go to high school. Angela and her family lived around the corner from us, less than a one minute walk from door to door, and had relatives living on their block much like our relatives living around us on our block. Little Angela's mother and my mother became friends when they were our Brownie Scout Troop leaders together and worked out the carpool schedule taking turns as our chauffeurs. My Dad never met anyone he didn't like, with the exception of all the boys who came to our house calling on either my sister or me. When my mother liked someone enough to socialize with them, which was not often, Dad had no problem having a good time.

I could see Little Angela taking in a large breath to say something in her nasal whine. "Br-a-a-a-n-dy, I want you to be my bri-i-i-i-desma-a-a-id," she said taking forever to drag out this request. I was already worn out from this five-minute visit so I knew I couldn't listen to this for an entire wedding and they hadn't even started all screaming at once.

Right after Mardi Gras I moved out of my parents' home and into one side of a shotgun double I share with my roommate Suzanne and the Schnauzers I rescued in

Mid City. My parents' house is in the Irish Channel about a fifteen-minute drive from Julia's guest house and my new home. I now had living expenses and quite frankly, I'd rather spend bridesmaid dress money on the dogs I rescue.

"As much as I would love to, Angela, I just moved out on my own and really don't have much money to buy the dress, shoes, and all that's required to be in a wedding party. How many bridesmaids are you having?" I started walking backwards toward the front door so I could make a fast exit before they could object. I wanted out of there before I got snagged by my mother into giving Little Angela a bridal shower. I'd rather poke myself in the eye with a pencil.

"Little A-A-An-gelo has five brothers and ten re-e-e-ally close cousins so we are gonna have fifte-e-e-e-n gr-o-o-o-msmen and thr-e-e-e-ushers." This took another two minutes off my life waiting for the total wedding party tally. There were going to be eighteen groomsmen, eighteen bridesmaids, both sets of parents, a couple of flower girls, a ring bearer, a maid of honor, and a matron (Angela's married cousin, Sofia). So far, I counted forty-five in the immediate wedding party before dates, husbands, wives or spouses with children and they all had children. The rehearsal party was going to look like a state dinner. I wondered how many photographers had wide-angle lens to accommodate a bridal army of this magnitude. I couldn't live through an entire wedding plan as Angela whined out every detail. I could always use the excuse I had to go home to walk the dogs if my visit spiraled much further into the dysfunctional realm of the usual family encounters. This conversation seemed like a one-way ticket headed there.

Angela was marrying a guy that weighed three hundred pounds and popped cannoli like breath mints. His head bubbled up from this great mass while his feet were stuck on short, massive legs that looked like they were holding up a ship in dry dock. His legs were perpetually on an angle under the great weight much like the Eiffel Tower's legs holding up the wide part of the iconic structure. His movements required great effort to hoist himself up, and put one thundering leg in front of the other. Often this effort was only employed to reach another plate of cannoli. Little Angela had been dating Little Angelo Tuddo since we all were in high school. Unlike men only being a junior, she was also a junior in the Italian sense, both named for a parent. He weighed the same then as he does now and would probably gain rather than lose weight for their wedding. In high school, Angela's twin brother started calling him Jabba the Hut, from Star Wars, because Angelo looked just like him. Little Tony said if Angela married him she would have little Jabba Hutt-ettes. Little Angela cried all through high school. What in the name of God could provoke anyone to date Jabba the Hut—let alone marry him? Big Angelo Tuddo, Little Angelo's dad, had ten car dealerships from the metro New Orleans area to Houston and Little Angela saw no limits on the American Express card he promised her as a wedding gift.

"Brandy, you have to stand for Little Angela. You two have been friends since grade school." My mother said, the recollection of my lifelong friendship with Angela returning. She gave me an eye-piercing stare over her half eyeglasses as if to exert mind control over my answer.

Every big, ugly, expensive bridesmaid dress flashed before my eyes. "I'll have to get back to you, Angela and right now I have to run home and let the dogs out. They've been cooped up all day! I'll call you tomorrow and let you know." I had reached the front door walking backwards.

"Brandy, you know, you gotta dance with me at the big Tuddo-rama wedding Angela's gonna have at The Veranda," yelled Little Tony in my ear as he ran up and grabbed me by the arm forcing me to stay. I could just picture dancing with Little Tony, since I was five foot eight and he was five foot five. He would have to put his head on my shoulder.

Miss Angela was yelling at Mr. Donnato asking how six hundred guests were going to all fit into the room at The Veranda when their maximum was four hundred fifty people.

My dad poured himself and Mr. Donnato another glass of wine from a bottle of Chianti. Then he walked over to me where I was struggling to get out of Little Tony's grip, raised his glass and announced, "Brandy's mother and I will gladly cover the cost for our daughter to stand in my friend Donnato's daughter's wedding."

Wait. What?

Little Tony added, "I guess that means you're in. I'm the best man but we won't be standing together, because you're too tall and I gotta take care of Nana getting in and outta the pew so you'll be standing with Angelo's friend from the neighborhood, your old squeeze, Dante."

Wait. What?

"Little Mickey, you'll be Angela's maid of honor," Mr. Donnato said. Angela and her mom beamed at me.

Thank God she didn't say anything. My mother was smiling, something that didn't happen often. "You gonna have a hundred boys wanna dance with you – a hundred Italian boys!"

This was moving way too fast. I had gone from graciously declining to now being the maid of honor?

Back slapping ensued among the men and hugging among the women. I was hugged into Miss Angela's huge bosoms while Mr. Donnato hoisted himself to his feet and stood in place while everyone came to him to slap him on the back or give him a hug. I stood in disbelief that now there was no way out of this mega wedding fiasco and Little Tony said I would be standing with Dante. It never occurred to me that Dante was friends with Angelo from school and might be at the wedding, let alone in the wedding party and I would be standing with him. This would make it interesting if I wanted to bring Jiff as my date. I left to go home, feed my dogs and tried not to imagine what fashion atrocity the bridesmaid dress had in store for me and seventeen of Little Angela's closest friends. Instead I decided to look forward to my date with Jiff on the first day of Jazz Fest tomorrow.

Chapter Seven

THE NEXT MORNING, Little Italy's wedding of the year was the last thing on my mind as I dressed for the day at Jazz Fest. It was a beautiful day with a clear blue sky and already hot. It was sure to feel like one hundred degrees in the shade so I wore a cotton gauze off-the-shoulder sundress to avoid tan lines. I brought my wide rimmed straw hat and put on my hammered gold earrings and bracelets. I dolled up just enough to look good spending the day with Jiff but still dressed casual and cool so I didn't melt in the African heat wave the Jazz Fest brought with it. I didn't mind the heat. I minded when it rained out the Fest and it turned into a mud wrestlers dream date. I'd rather be hot than muddy. Today was a cloudless, sweltering day – just the way I liked it.

Jiff had the pricey VIP package, so we drove right onto the Fairgrounds, parked and breezed through the line that normally took thirty minutes to get through. I could get used to this preferred treatment. To meet two of his friends, Jiff and I made our way through the crowd to the flagpole, which was centrally located inside the racetrack. The problem was all twenty thousand people had the same meeting place. This was the predetermined meeting place for everyone who attended the Jazz Fest and planned to hook up inside. We picked a place and one of us would walk around and see if we could find our friends. We'd wait ten minutes and if they didn't show we'd try again in two hours. This was our agreed-to plan. So far, they were a no show and it was no surprise. It was a record-breaking crowd for Friday, and Jimmy Buffet was the closing act this evening.

On top of the crowds, it was blistering hot. Jiff bought me water in a bottle so I could refill it and splash myself from time to time. We strolled around the fest grabbing a beer and treating ourselves to Crawfish Monica, my favorite fest food. We meandered over to stake out our special spot to catch Jimmy along the racetrack's inside rail, about two hundred feet from the stage on a sloping incline of ground that gave us an advantage looking over the sea of people waiting for our favorite parrot head.

My other favorite, Irma Thomas, was about to start her performance so I could stand here for the remainder of the day and catch the two performers I came to see. Jiff and I had the same taste in local music and performers. We often went to the French Quarter to hear an artist or band we liked and would spent a large part of the night dancing.

"Wait here, I'm going to get another beer. You want anything?" he said into my ear over the music starting up.

"I'll take another bottle of water if it's at the beer booth. Don't wait in two lines," I said back to him in his ear. This put us in very close proximity to each other's lips and his found mine, giving me a lingering see-you-in-a-few-minutes lip lock.

Jiff walked off in search of a short beer line and an even shorter bathroom line when my skin started to crawl and I felt the presence of Little Tony slithering up next to me.

"So that's your new squeeze?" He spoke in rhythm with this wise-guys' bouncing thing he had going on. Problem was Little Tony wanted everyone to think he was a wise guy but he wasn't even clever, let alone, wise.

"Yes, he is. Now go away."

"Too bad you're with him today or we could, you know, hang out. Are you bringing him to the wedding?" He kept bouncing, unwrapping a stick of Wrigley's gum, and then putting the pack in his pocket without offering me a piece.

"I haven't decided. It depends on how ugly the bridesmaids' dresses are and how bad I look in it," I said without thinking. Luckily, Little Tony didn't care how anyone looked in the dresses, only if he could get a bridesmaid out of one.

"You know, Angela's gonna have two really, really good bands, and, uh, you know, we could dance up a storm, you and me, if you don't bring a date." He pimp-bounced out this easy to refuse offer in time with the gum chewing.

"Really, two bands?"

"Yeah, dat's right. The first band is for everyone, you know, that blows off the church part and gets there early. Dat band is gonna play until the wedding party finishes with the photos upstairs, and band number two will start when Angela and my dad dance their father/daughter dance. Then, they play for the rest of the reception."

"What two bands did they choose?" I asked, wanting him to keep talking so I didn't have to say anything to him. I was thinking that none of the band members from Julia's fiasco had yet to return calls to the investigator or Julia about their dead band member, last I'd heard.

"One of them is playing here today, the Levee Men, you know, they play up and down the Mississippi. You know, and…"

"The Levee Men—the don't-hold-anything-back band?" I cut Little Tony off. This was the name of the band we were trying to find. "Do you know them or how to get in touch with them?" My skin was getting prickly at the thought that I could follow up with them and ask about Guitarzan's habits and friends.

"Yeah, you know, I can hook you up." His head was starting to look like one of those plastic bobble dogs. I had to stop looking at him. I didn't want to get a headache in this heat.

"You can? When? Right now? Do it, right now. Call them on your cell so I can talk to someone right now." My heart was racing at the thought of asking them some specific questions about Julia's dilemma.

"You some kinda nutso fan? Why you gotta talk to them right now?"

"Just do it, please?" I smiled.

"So, you know, I do this for you, you gonna dance with me, right, at the wedding?

Jiff returned just as Little Tony was about to make the call. He had a big grin on his handsome face and was holding two VIP All-Access passes.

"I really want to go see The Levee Men if we can get to their tent," I said to Jiff. "Never mind that call, we'll just go over there," I said to Little Tony and put my hand on his stopping him from making the call on his cell phone.

"I'll see ya' at the, you know, wedding." Little Tony was yelling the bounce talk at my back.

"What wedding? When?" asked Jiff.

"My childhood friend, Angela, I went all through school with is getting married. The rest of her family is really very nice. That was her goofy brother and he makes my skin crawl."

"Am I going to be, you know, your date." He was making fun of Little Tony and bounced when he talked, bobbing his head up and down like a bobble head doll.

I was laughing when I said, "I don't know. I'll decide after I see what dress Angela picks out for us." I put my arm through his and my head on his shoulder. He was tall, just the right height for me and he kissed the top of my head. "I'm not sure if I want you to see me in whatever dress I'll be forced to wear."

"You'll be the prettiest girl there, no matter what you have to wear," he said.

IT WAS A record crowd and in this heat no one was moving fast so it took awhile to get across the inside field of the track to the very opposite end where the Levee Men were playing. Jiff flashed the all too wonderful ALL ACCESS VIP PASS and Security lifted the rope and allowed us to enter backstage. We were offered soft drinks, alcohol, beer, wine, and a variety of snacks. A sushi chef was on hand preparing trays, which were being scarfed up as fast as he could roll it out. Jiff got our drinks and then we were directed to sit in an area on the stage to the side of the performers.

This was heaven.

I took this time to inform Jiff why I really wanted to see and speak to these guys if time allowed. He was fine with it. We both knew of and liked their music and this way we could have a little howdy time before I started grilling them on the habits of their missing guitar player. After the band members came onstage, they tuned up a few minutes then came over to socialize with the fans in the VIP section. We introduced ourselves, telling them we were fans and enjoyed their music. The singer, who said his name was Maurice, looked at me and said, "Really, your name, your real name is Brandy Alexander? You're not an entertainer, are you?"

I smiled and told him the brief story how my dad and his brother waited in a bar for me the night I was born and came up with the name they thought just seem fitting with the last name of Alexander for a New Orleans girl.

"It's not even her favorite cocktail," Jiff said laughing. "But, now it's mine." He put his arm around me and gave me one of his adoring looks.

I saw a guitar player taking extra time tuning up. "New guitar player?" I nodded toward the new guy.

"Yeah, we lost a good friend and band member right before this gig," said the lead singer, Maurice. "We almost thought we'd have to cancel playing the Fest but this guy has played with us in the past so he knows our set."

"Sorry to hear that," answered Jiff for both of us and I realized this was a clue to give it some time before I pressed on. I wasn't going to bring up being friends with Julia and where Guitarzan bought it until the band could see we were on their side. I'm sure the band, like the police, were convinced Julia was guilty and all that was left to do was schedule her lethal injection.

"Well, Miss Brandy Alexander, I'm going to dedicate our first love song we play today to you and this guy. Y'all look great together." To Jiff he said, "That's a hot babe you got there. In fact, come to our after party tonight. I'll have our manager give you a couple of passes." I gave him the same big smile I gave Little Tony. Sometimes a girl's gotta do what a girl's gotta do. He waved at his manager, held up two fingers, pointed to us, then he walked over to rally the band to gear up for their set. Now we were invited to a party where I could talk to all of the band members and see who knew what.

Chapter Eight

"**W**OW, I'D LOVE to go with you to Le Petit tonight with your extra ticket. You know how I love the theatre but I already have plans. Jiff had the all access pass at Jazz Fest and we were invited by the lead singer of The Levee Men to their party tonight," I told Julia over the phone.

"Well, Miss La Tee Da," Julia said. "I'll look for your photo on the society page."

"I don't think so, but this is good for you. This is the band your dead guy played in."

"I'm painfully aware of who they are since they cancelled their reservations after Gervais, well, you know," she snipped. Julia had a one way view of the world, and that was the world according to Julia."

"Cancelled? I think you were in jail and the police along with the crime scene people wouldn't let them check in," I said.

"Well, that might have had something to do with it, sure."

"Well, Julia, even though the world is against you, I am still on your side." I was glad she couldn't see the eye roll I added. "I want to see what they know or at least find out if he met up or had problems with anyone here. You should be thanking me. I think this evens the score from when I asked you to wear that gorilla suit to help me sneak into the hospital and talk to Jiff the night he was shot."

"Help me get past this ordeal and, yes, that score is settled. I'm terrified this is now so out of control. I really appreciate you standing by me and having my back. Most people are looking at me like I'm going to bash their head in. The cops aren't investigating any further. They think I'm guilty and that's that. They're just waiting for the trial."

"Well, I know you didn't do it and Jiff got one of his female investigators an invite to come along with us tonight to this party. You know, bands will never say no to bringing an extra girl to a party. She will snoop around and see if she comes up with anything."

"Thanks. Let me know if y'all find out anything," she said, then hung up.

Y Y Y

JIFF AND I arrived with his female private investigator, Michelle, at The Oak Leaf Bar about 10:30 p.m. and security barely looked at the passes before waving us in. The bar was crowded with the eclectic group of normal patrons, the uptown crowd who liked live music and had been loyal followers since their college days, college kids from Tulane and Loyola, musicians and Levee Men fans or guests. The cool thing about The Oak Leaf was that peoples' paths crossed with decades of age differences to dance to funky New Orleans music, sometimes until dawn. The common denominator was fun and music. Jiff pulled me by the hand out to the dance floor and Michelle went to work. She was a cutie. She had a pixie haircut, big eyes and a fashion model's face. Jiff said she could sell snow to an Eskimo. It wasn't long before she

The drummer added, "My money's on 'ole Violet having something to do with it."

"Yeah, bummer." The bass player shook his head and sat with his eyes closed playing air guitar.

"Find Violet and you might find some answers," Maurice said.

"Is that her real name?" I said to no one in particular. "She didn't show up here tonight? It seems she would want to share some time with his friends."

"Well, that's what we know her as and she didn't come here tonight because she knows we don't like her. She knew Gervais' soft spot, which was drugs, and she exploited it. He was a good guitar player when he was straight. That means, when she wasn't around. Too bad she didn't run off with that weirdo that followed her everywhere. If Violet was actually in the band, that would have made that guy her groupie," the drummer said to the keyboard player. "But, us not liking her, or the skinny guy following her or us around, never kept her from stalking Gervais and bringing him what he could not refuse—cocaine. I bet she knows he's dead. I think your girlfriend keeps her informed." He air quoted the word informed when the keyboard player's girlfriend left the table for the ladies room.

"My girlfriend stopped associating with Violet or *Violent*, as she now calls her, after she drugged our dog and it died. Violet wouldn't admit to it, but the vet said it was given Rohypnol, you know, roofies. Rumor is the skinny guy who followed Violet was her drug connection. We think he's the one who slipped it to a gal or two at one of the places we've played, I guess he was hoping to get lucky since Violet was all into Gervais. We think that's where she got it," the keyboard player said to the group.

"My girlfriend still gets upset over our dog so she leaves whenever Violet's name comes up." Then, he said, "Violet is a waffle waitress at Pancake Paddy on Canal or she was the last I heard."

"You think this woman killed your dog?" I was almost out of my seat when Jiff grabbed my thigh by way of holding me down and sending the 'not the time or the place' message.

"Not just our dog, but the neighbor's dog also. Same thing happened to their pet about a week before our dog. We didn't think it was Violet until she was staying with us when our dog died."

I could hardly stay in my seat. I wanted to find this woman and pound her. What kind of person gives drugs to someone's pet? "Pancake Paddy? Isn't that close to the end of Canal by the cemeteries?" I asked.

"Yeah, right. Most of us are from all over south Louisiana and don't have relatives to crash with here so we were supposed to stay at that new B&B near it until Gervais was killed."

Y Y Y

JIFF SPENT THE night at my apartment. It was early Saturday morning when we got in and we stretched out on the floor, my head on his shoulder and discussed what we'd discovered over the course of the day and evening we spent together. We fell asleep like that. We woke up when my dogs stretched and shook themselves awake. When we didn't get up immediately, they barked, pounced on us, licked and playfully nipped at our ears.

"Boy, they're better than an alarm clock," Jiff said.

Just then I heard the key in the front door and my

roommate, Suzanne came in. I made some quick introductions. Suzanne looked dead on her feet.

"Nice to meet you, but you have to excuse me, I worked all night and have classes this afternoon so I really need to get some sleep. Later," she said as she drifted off to her bedroom.

I explained Suzanne and I grew up on the same block and I moved in with her right after I met him. She worked nights and I worked days and we rarely saw each other except when she came in sometimes. It was the perfect arrangement. It felt like living alone but having someone to split the rent with.

Jiff made breakfast while I fed three Schnauzers, my dog Meaux Jeaux and two rescues I was currently trying to find homes for. He fixed us scrambled eggs while I dished out the bowls of food in my doggie soup kitchen.

"Who takes care of Isabella if you don't go home?" I asked.

"You remember Sam, our security guard? Of course you do, he adopted one of your Schnauzers. He takes Isabella for a sleepover with Einstein. Those two dogs love each other. I guess it's professional courtesy since they're both Schnauzers and Isabella isn't too friendly with other dogs."

Jiff was breaking pieces of bagel off to give to the three pair of eyes staring at him when they started barking at a knock on the kitchen door. When I opened it, there on the other side of the screen was Dante. He went white with anger when he saw Jiff at the stove with the skillet.

"Seems I caught you at a bad time," was all he could spit out.

"No, not really, do you want to come in?" I asked trying to push open the screen door. Dante put his hand on it and kept it closed.

"Call me later if you want this info I have on Julia's tox screen," he added, "if you're interested." He spun around going down the back stairs and around the side of the house to the front where he'd parked. I took off after him.

"Wait. Of course I'm interested in her tox screen. This isn't what you think," I said sprinting down the driveway behind him. He, stopped abruptly, turned, and I ran smack into him. He had his arms around me for a second as I slammed into his chest. When we both realized we had our arms around each other, he pushed me back, dropping his like I was on fire.

"How do you know what I think? Besides, you have a guest. Shouldn't you go back to...entertain him?" The vein in his neck was pumping blood to his face and the white was turning redder with every breath.

"Not that I owe you an explanation, and you showed up unannounced," I said, mustering some degree of indignation. He turned to start leaving again, but I grabbed the back of his shirt. "We don't even date and I'm not obligated to you or you to me in any way. But just so you know, I didn't sleep with him. I mean, I didn't have sex with him. We just fell asleep on the floor after a late night." I spilled this out in one nervous breath while my heart raced. Then I let go of his shirt.

We both stood there a minute before he turned around, held out the folder in his hand. "Here's a copy of both tox screens. They both had alcohol in their blood. St. Germain had higher levels than Julia but both had traces of Rohypnol. He might have gotten some in his own drink when he tried to drug her. They both were pretty bombed, from what this report says."

I took it from him. "She didn't kill that guy but does this report help her?" I scanned the report. Dante just stood there looking at the folder in my hands. "I thought this drug rendered you more or less paralyzed if you were slipped it."

"The Coroner's office says it's inconclusive. The glasses were both rinsed out and we never found a wine bottle to see if it was in the bottle or just put in the glass." He paused before looking me in the face. "I can't watch you with another man. I can't do it." He left me standing alone in my driveway feeling hollow and empty inside.

🍸 🍸 🍸

I HANDED JIFF the folder with Julia's report in it and we ate breakfast discussing what might happen with the results. He said, "That was nice of your friend to bring this by."

"Actually, that was huge for Dante. He hates Julia."

"But, he likes you and it seems he didn't expect to see me here. You two have some history together?" Jiff tried to sound casual but he was fishing. He didn't know about Dante and I hadn't had any reason to bring it up. I figured when and if he asked, I'd tell him. Well, now he was asking.

"Our history is we lived next door to each other. I've known him forever. It seems our parents thought we were going to get married…eventually." I looked at the report in his hands. "Dante told me the coroner says the report is inconclusive," I said.

"Was he the cop that was standing near you the night I kissed you at the parade?" he asked.

"Yes, but it wasn't Dante that made you move along,

it was his partner. What about this report? Does it help Julia or hurt her?" I really wanted to get off the subject of Dante and me.

"Inconclusive does not mean inadmissible," Jiff added, reading through it again. "If she was drugged by the guy, maybe she can plead self defense if she was aware he was trying to rape her. Maybe one drugged the other, since both had scant traces of the chemical. The one who planned it could have gotten some in his or her own glass since the alcohol levels might have influenced his or her motor skills."

"I really hope you don't use that as a defense. Julia will be raked over the coals for being in his room and her sex life—the many, many details—will be used against her. She didn't drug anybody, why would she? And he didn't have to drug a willing partner in Julia. She slept in his room for God's sake. Julia is a lot of things, but I do not believe she murdered him."

"What made her pick up with a guy like St. Germain? He seems a little rough around the edges for Julia," Jiff said.

"Even though I should not speak ill of the dead, St. Germain was a prince next to her drunken loser of a husband who almost burned her house down. All she did was kick him out. Julia does not have good judgment when it comes to men. Have you met Frank?"

Jiff finished breakfast and cleaned up my kitchen, washed all the dishes and put them away before we walked to the front door. After a tight hug and kiss that should have been saying I'll see you later instead of hell-o-o-o-o to my girly parts, he added, "Look, that guy clearly doesn't think he's out of your life. Just let him know that now I'm in your life until you tell me I'm not."

Chapter Nine

THE ENTIRE BRIDAL party was there cackling like chickens when I arrived, fifteen minutes late, to meet Angela and the others at Wedding World—*With All Things White and Wonderful for your Wedding!* This place was the size of the Wal-Mart warehouse on Veterans Highway in Metairie, with every conceivable ugly bridesmaid's dress under one enormous roof. Its only competition in terms of size and tackiness was the Mardi Gras float den on the West Bank.

Every saleswoman in the place was commandeered to bring armloads of dresses through a heart shaped doorway into the fitting suite where Angela, her mother, her grandmother—who spoke no English, only Italian—and the other seventeen bridesmaids were waiting. Our job today was to try on dresses until Angela picked one she thought we all looked good in. Each selection was a fashion faux pas. The ones with empire waists made us all look pregnant. The body hugging, tight fitting ones made the not-so-skinny girls look like snakes that swallowed a watermelon. Not one dress was flattering to two of us at any time, let alone all eighteen of us.

"What color did she pick for us to wear?" I asked the girl closest to me.

"We each get to wear our favorite color in the dress she finally decides on," the girl advised before blowing a big bubble with her gum and popping it. Then she proceeded to pull it off her face with her fingers and stick the gum back into her mouth to continue chewing it.

"Are there that many colors in the spectrum?" I asked. "I think we will exhaust the color wheel before everyone picks her favorite." I worked my way next to Angela and said I wanted to wear a black dress.

"Bla-a-a-ck? For a w-e-e-e-dding? No, Brandy, you can't wear bla-a-a-ack," she whined as her mother stood up and started to wring her hands. Nana directed her fierce stare at me.

"You never heard of a black and white wedding? Angela, you would really stand out as the only one in white with the men in black tuxedos and the girls all in black dresses. Besides, who can't use a little black dress again?" I was working hard to sell this idea, hoping Angela would see herself as the ultimate center of attention being the only one in white. I had a mental flash of me wearing a hoop skirt, and a poof-sleeved, puce or mustard-colored dress making me look like a three-day-old dead fish. "You could have the tablecloths at the reception all in black and you would stand out everywhere you went surrounded by everyone in black, after-five attire. Your invitations can say it's a black and white wedding and then your guests will know to wear black. I saw a wedding like that and no one could stop looking at the bride."

"Gee-e-e-e-z, I don't kn-o-o-o-w."

I thought I had her seeing the big picture when Angela's mother started speaking in rapid Italian to Angela's grandmother telling her of my idea. The permanent scowl on the old lady's face dug deeper into her wrinkles as Angela's mother explained. She looked at everyone with a fierce scowl or a not-so-fierce scowl, which she saved for

Angela. Nana stiffened in the plush chair, the only chair in this room, then shook her head three times while she scissored her hands back and forth in a definite, no, No, NO.

"Ok, then. I want to wear blue." I said.

"Well, all r-i-i-i-ght. Everyb o-o-o-dy, Bra-a-a-ndy is we-a-a-a-ring blu-u-u-e."

Angela's nasal announcement gave her enough time to pull out a tablet and start a list of what colors the others wanted. Then the fighting began. Five others wanted blue. It continued on and on around Angela, Angela's mother and Nana as sales ladies measured and fitted everyone for her dress size so Angela could pick the one dress that made all of us look equally bad next to her. The sales women moved around the room making notes on our sizes for alterations in between toting armloads of wedding gowns in for Angela between our fittings. We had to stop each and every time Angela came out in yet another dress to *ooh* and *ah* while her mother and grandmother cried, hugged each other then threw their hands in the air shouting something in Italian. I felt like I was trapped in a bad Fellini movie.

This enormous waste of my afternoon culminated in a hideous choice of a long poof-sleeved ball gown type dress with a hoop skirt, in blue. It made me look like a tidal wave. The fat girls looked fat and even the skinny ones looked fat in yards of swooshing peau de soie. My skin crawled every time someone's fingernail ran down the fabric. The good news about wearing this dress, if there was any, would be if I did ask Jiff to the wedding and had to stand with Dante as the groomsman, the hoop skirt would mean neither one of them could get close enough to me to bother the other one. I fantasized about the future of my dress cut into dust rags or used for stuffing in dog beds.

For her dress, Angela selected a strapless, tight fitting mermaid tail-wedding gown with a tiara instead of a veil. Angela and her mother were all smiles while Nana had the not-so-fierce scowl going on. The army of flower girls being escorted by the cute little boys in tuxedos would also wear miniature-wedding gowns and they would look darling in these.

The bridesmaids were about to revolt. We descended on Angela like sharks on bleeding prey. No one could ever wear these dresses again, anywhere, except the gal who got stuck with the orange one. Maybe she could wear it to a prison gala should she ever find herself in the big house. Angela stood her ground with her mother and Nana as her backup. Several threatened to drop out and Angela's mother started wringing her hands again. Three said they couldn't afford a dress they would never be able to wear anywhere else again. They were the hot pink, mustard yellow and lime green colors. No one wanted to put a deposit on the dress to be ordered. Finally, Angela made a decision and mandated we would all wear the same color—the green one.

Wait. What? I hate green. It's my least favorite color and I look dead in it.

Bubble-gum girl popped another one while Nana gave her the fierce look. The faces on the eighteen of us didn't change much and that was it as far as Angela was willing to give in since this was 'her' big day, and we weren't the bride and 'she' was the one we were all supposed to be there for. The green she chose was a weird one, close to the color of a rotting avocado. Great, we would all look bad together. I calculated the yardage needed for eighteen dresses and thought we could rid the planet of this color. Who would loom this much of a hideous, unflattering hue? If I looked at it this way, maybe I would feel that I was doing good instead of contributing to the visual ugliness of the world. If I had to say anything nice about the dress, and this was a stretch, it would have to be that the sweetheart neckline showed a lot of cleavage and even made the flat-chested girls look good.

I tapped my watch when I caught Angela's eye across the room of partially dressed bridesmaids waiting to be fitted, pointed to the door and blew her a kiss with a big smile. I had to escape before I lost patience and wanted to strangle someone trying to be helpful in this wedding wonderland. One of the sales commandos handed me a color swatch and claim check for the dress, and told me to go to the shoe department where I could order my size and have it dyed to match the dress. Oh great, now a pair of shoes in this color I'll never wear. The bubble-popper and another bridesmaid made the escape when I did.

I was the first to finish in the shoe department when I heard the other girl mention to bubble gum-girl we had to go to the hat department next.

A hat? I was just about to ask what kind of a hat when bubble gum girl answered, "Yeah, it's the only good part of this outfit. Angela picked out an anti-bellum hat."

"I think you mean ante-bellum," the elegant, well-dressed sales lady said trying to correct her.

"Dat's what I said, an anti-bellum hat." Bubble gum rolled her eyes and the sales lady graciously moved to help the next girl in line.

A big hat? Great. Now at this blasted reception I would be stuck wearing a hat the size of a satellite dish all night, because once you put on a hat you can't take it off or you will have hat hair. This entire ensemble was like date repellant and would run off anyone trying to intrude into my personal space. I'd have at least a four-foot diameter around me until I undressed.

Dancing at the wedding was going to be a real challenge unless the only one asking me was Little Tony. He would fit under the hat.

As my luck would have it, I wore the sample size they had in stock. The sales lady said this was great for me since I didn't need to order one and pay for alterations, I could take it home with me today. Oh joy!

Trying to get the dress with that enormous hoop skirt into the trunk of my car reminded me of trying to get the Jack back in the Box. The hoop underskirt made the hood bounce up every time I tried to close it. The dress and all that came with it was tap dancing on my last nerve and I considered tying it to my bumper and dragging it behind my cute little BMW. I finally wedged it into the backseat. It completely obliterated my rearview window. The hat got the place of honor in the front seat and had to ride on a forty-five degree angle, obstructing the passenger window view.

I drove to Julia's to share the tox screen info Dante had given me. While it wasn't great news, Jiff thought it was good news and she needed something to keep her spirits up. Frank was more of a glass half empty kinda guy and his reminding her constantly that she could go to prison was making Julia paranoid and depressed.

They were in the garden and Julia was directing Frank how she wanted the shrubs groomed. Julia was moving around like a zombie. Frank was on a stepladder with a hedge clipper trying to get Julia's attention for approval. "What's that in your backseat?" he asked as I got out of my car in front of Julia's B&B. He dropped the hedge clipper to the ground, turned with his back to the ladder and came down the steps like a Rockette in a stage production.

"Only the most beautiful dress in the world I wanted y'all to see," I said. This got Julia's attention and Frank had already opened the car door and was tugging the hoop-shaped hanging bag out of its confinement.

"What do you have in here? What's this big round thing?" Frank looked like he was in a fight for his life with the dress trying to get it out the back seat. For me it didn't want to go into the car and for Frank, it didn't want to come out.

"What kinda dress comes in a round hanging bag?" asked Julia. "Wait. Are you in a wedding?" She spotted the Wedding World insignia stamped on the bag.

"Nothing gets by you, Eagle Eye." This got a smile from Julia. "And, yes, I'm in the biggest Italian wedding of the decade."

Frank held the dress bag at arms length, not wanting to drop it but clearly trying to detach himself from it. He said, "This is a bridesmaid dress?" with all the distaste his voice and facial expression could muster. "You are wearing a bridesmaid's dress that has a hoop skirt?" Frank and Julia looked at each other by way of confirming what they both thought.

"Yes."

"Well, come on inside and put that sucker on. I wanna see this," Julia said as her face broke into a full smile.

Frank offered to button me up since the dang dress had at least one hundred covered buttons and loops to go around each one, not buttonholes or a zipper. This took several minutes during which I had to endure their remarks on how this dress would be like birth control, since it took so long to get in or out of it, my partner would lose interest or die from waiting. Frank admitted he was only buttoning every other one to go faster. When I turned around to show them the dress, they both doubled over laughing.

"Why, Scarlett, I love what you've done with the drapes!" Frank said with his hand on his hip and waving the other one around over his head.

"When did you agree to buy Betsy Ross' dress and be in a Civil War reenactment of a wedding?" asked Julia, hardly able to get the words out through her laughter.

Frank was standing there holding the hat. "Do you want to put this on for the whole effect?" he asked.

"No, because I want you both surprised when you see me in the wedding with it and the basket of flowers I have to carry."

"Basket?" Frank looked at Julia again.

"Not just a basket, but a bushel basket, big enough to put a bale of cotton in," I said.

Frank was bent in half again laughing at how ridiculous I was going to look.

"That is the same response this dress got from the other seventeen bridesmaids at Wedding World," I said.

"Eighteen bridesmaids? Are you kidding?" Julia was laughing so hard I could barely make out the questions.

"Look, Frank, she is going to have to hold her arm straight out to the side to even touch the guy she's standing with to escort her down the aisle. Who are you stuck standing with?" she asked to more raucous laughter.

"Dante," I said. They both stopped laughing. I guess Julia briefed Frank on the Dante situation.

"What? Why are you standing in a wedding and why are you standing with Dante, and why is he standing in the same wedding with you, and is he wearing the Confederate or Yankee uniform? I bet he's a Yankee. He would be. I'll shoot him myself if he is wearing a Yankee uniform." Julia took a breath and was about to launch into another series of questions I wouldn't be able to answer fast enough when I held up my hands for her to stop.

"I knew you'd get a kick out of this circus tent I have to wear but I really came over here to bring you some news Dante gave me early this morning." I pulled out the report and gave it to her as Frank helped me out of the dress, leaving me standing there in my hoop and underwear. He motioned for me to remove the hoop and said he would find a place to hang my dress upstairs so it wouldn't get wrinkled. He ran off somewhere with it and I really thought he was going to try it on himself.

"Why did you see Dante early in the morning? What was he doing at your house...early?" Julia asked, more suspicious of his visit than the actual reason he came by, i.e. the report in my hand.

"Let's concentrate on this report. I know you didn't kill that guy and while this confirms it to me, Jiff says it's not conclusive. It also shows trace amounts of roofies in Gervais' blood along with a ton of alcohol in both of your screens."

"I don't know what to believe anymore. That night after we got back here is a blur to me. Maybe I did hit him if I thought he was trying to rape me. I don't remember anything like that, but why else would I have hit him in the head? I remember I liked him and I thought he was good looking in that bohemian— musician—bad boy sort of way," she said, then more sheepishly she added, "I was thinking of going to bed with him. He wouldn't have had to force himself on me."

"I told you, don't say that again—ever—out loud in front of anyone. If we get called to testify and they ask us if you ever said you think you did it, we'd have to say yes. I think ole Guitarzan slipped you a Mickey," I said.

"Well, he might have slipped himself one too since he poured himself a glass and drank along with me. I was fine and so was he until we got back here," Julia said.

"You said he had the bottle in his room already that night? He didn't buy it along the way?"

"Yeah, that's right. I went to get two wine glasses and a corkscrew because he showed me the bottle…said a friend gave it to him. He said it was a really good bottle of red wine and he talked me into trying a glass with him. I really had had enough to drink that night, but he was right, it was very good, or at least what I remember of it."

"Well, that makes me think he didn't know what was in it if he drank it too. Did he say the name of this friend?" I asked.

"No, but when he told me I got the distinct impression it was an ex from the way he carefully spoke about seeing his friend that day, before he checked in, and he caught himself once referring to his friend as a 'she'."

"Are you sure it's the same friend? The ex doesn't sound like she'd give him a bottle of wine to enjoy with someone else. I hope you told all this to the attorney in Jiff's office handling your case."

"Yes, of course. I just feel so out on a limb here. Part of me wants to blame myself because it's my place of business where it happened. The cops are doing a bang up job letting the media believe it too."

"I don't think Dante believes you did it," I said. "And you know he would really like to." I added smiling. We both knew Dante and Julia were not simpatico. Dante blamed Julia for being instrumental in our breakup and he hadn't liked her much even before that.

"Dante just wants you back to the way things were. He could care less what happens to me and the only reason he appears to be helping is so he can get close to you. You're not thinking of going back with him now that you see how the other half lives, are you? Your new guy adores you. I wish I had someone who looked at me the way he looks at you every time you walk in the room."

"Julia, I'm not sure what I want." I couldn't believe what just came out of my mouth. I thought I was happy moving on, but the look on Dante's face when he saw Jiff in my kitchen this morning touched me to my core and now it was playing over and over in my head. "Dante brought this to me without me asking him, and saw Jiff there making me breakfast. Your attorney would have gotten it anyway."

"Whoa, Cowgirl. Back up to the part where Jiff was making you breakfast. So-o-o-o, things are moving along?" Julia's big grin had me uncomfortable and I was trying to decide just how much to tell her.

Chapter Ten

I WENT INTO my office early Monday since I had a lot to catch up on after taking two days off last week, one getting Julia out of jail and Friday to go to The Fest with Jiff. My voicemail was full and not accepting any more messages so I set about clearing that up. The secretary informed me that two DEA guys were there and asked if I could meet with them. They had subpoenas for my office to pull the phone records of several people to see who called them on their birthdays. Even drug dealers call their mothers on Mother's Day and birthdays. The subpoenas were for phone records of mothers and/or girlfriends of drug dealers and felony murder suspects. The DEA wanted to see if they could get a lead on where some of them might be located by investigating the calls made to their women on their birthdays.

When they left I called Dante and told him what the DEA wanted and asked him why didn't the police get a subpoena for Julia's phone records to see who made calls to her leading up to the murder. I told him about Julia remembering a woman calling without leaving her name. I said it might be a jilted girlfriend, or his ex-girlfriend who might know who he met up with when he came to town.

"Why isn't Julia's big attorney..." he paused and I knew he wanted to link Jiff to me but then thought better of it, "...asking for the phone records?"

"I don't know and I guess I can call him and suggest it. I could pull them and look at them, but I don't want my inappropriate discovery to negatively impact the results if this can help Julia, and I really think it would shed some light on who was calling and looking for him. Besides, I don't want to lose my job. Who would feed my dogs?"

"I'll pull them but you do know they go right into evidence no matter what?" There was a pause and then he sounded like the Dante I grew up with when he added, "I'd feed your dogs."

"Yes, but I really believe there might be something there to help her or cast doubt. Thank you for feeding my dogs if I wind up in the pokey." There were a few moments of awkward silence where I tried to figure out what to say next. Dante was the first to break it.

"If you meet me this evening for a drink, I'll tell you what I find. I can't give you anything written. Her attorney will have to subpoena the info or get it in discovery." Then he paused again briefly before he added, "You're probably busy tonight."

"No, I'm not busy tonight. I was just trying to decide where to meet you and what time. I have to pick up a little rescue from the vet who is going to his new home tomorrow but I can meet you after I let the dogs out and feed them. Is 6:00 or 6:30 after work O.K. with you?"

"Make it 6:30 so you have enough time and I'll meet you at Napoleon House." Dante knew this was my favorite spot in the French Quarter to have a cocktail and dinner.

"O.K. I'll see you there… and Dante, thanks."

"Don't thank me until you see what I find." He hung

up.

Y Y Y

WHEN I WALKED into the Napoleon House, Dante was sitting at the bar waiting. He stood up when he saw me and pulled the bar stool next to him out for me. He was drinking a beer and I was about to order, when a dark rum and tonic with three limes showed up before me. It always made me feel good when he anticipated exactly what I wanted. He wasn't much of a talker, definitely more of a doer.

This felt so comfortable, the way we were before that parade kiss with Jiff, meeting after work to discuss our day. I'm sure neither of us knew what topics were off limits. Soon, we were laughing and smiling at each other. He pulled out his notebook and told me what he found out regarding the phone records.

"It seems the number that left the message was a local 504 number. I looked it up to see who it belonged to. The call was made from a pay phone inside Pancake Paddy about 6:00 p.m. the night St. Germain checked in. The other blocked calls were from a cell phone that originated in the same cell tower with the 225 area code. The lab said it would take a few days to see if they could ID that cell number."

I said, "The dead guy was a band member in The Levee Men. His ex-girlfriend worked at Pancake Paddy right up the street from the Bed and Breakfast. It might be a good idea to talk to her. One of the band members said her name is Violet Fornet. I don't know anymore about her but the band members who played with the dead guy might. I bumped into one of your fellow groomsmen in the wedding at Jazz Fest, Little Tony, who told me The Levee Men were playing that day. I went to talk to them backstage."

"Steer clear of that idiot. I'd like to strangle him."

"Little Tony? He's a goof, but harmless, besides you're a fellow groomsman of his in the big wedding, aren't you? It might not look good for you to kill him."

"Yeah? Maybe they'll kick me out and I won't have to stand in it."

"If that happens, tell them I helped you strangle him so I'll get booted out too." We both laughed, but I seemed more amused than Dante.

"Why are you and I standing together, if Little Tony is the Best Man?" Dante asked me.

"Have you met the grandmother with the permanent scowl on her face?" I asked him.

"No, why?"

"Angela said even though Little Tony is the best man, someone has to escort Nana up and down the aisle, and in and out of the pew. Angela's mother, Miss Angela, decided Little Tony had to escort Nana around so she doesn't fall and she can keep up with the rest of the wedding party. Since all the other groomsmen are Italian, and short, that leaves you as the only one tall enough to stand with me," I said.

"You're kidding, right?"

"I might have to like Nana because of this," I said laughing.

We finished our drinks and he asked if I'd join him for dinner. There was a table for two waiting for us in the corner in the smaller dining room. There were no tables close to us and it felt very private. Dante sat with his back to the wall and I sat to his left, not across from him. We both had a phobia about sitting with our backs to the door, his probably from police training and I probably got mine from him. It did make us sit closer together rather than across from each other.

"This is very nice, us here having a drink and dinner. I miss catching up with you after our day," I said. Dante had ordered a bottle of wine, which was waiting at the table for us.

"I miss you, us, too. I know I'm not very open with the way I'm feeling about things but we've known each other forever, Brandy."

"Yes, we have. I'm afraid everyone, our parents—both sets—had such great expectations for us that we didn't know if it was what we wanted."

"I always knew I wanted you. Us."

I'm not sure what I was expecting but I wasn't expecting a new, romantic Dante to be wooing me on a date. I started to feel a little guilty like I was cheating on Jiff when Saturday morning I had felt like I was cheating on Dante when he came by my house to drop the report.

"I'm glad we got some things out in the open," I said. "I don't like not talking with you and not being nice to each other. No matter what happens we should always be friends."

"I want more than nice, and I don't want to be friends. I'm willing to work to get you back," he said, taking my hands on the table.

"What about your partner, Hanky? I don't want to mess up anything you might have going on there," I said feeling rotten, like I was cheating with her boyfriend out to dinner.

"I don't know what you heard about the two of us, but whatever it is, it's probably not true," Dante answered me and squeezed my hands. "Don't worry about that."

Great, for years I couldn't get one guy to commit to me about anything and now I had two men who were professing their undying love.

Well, sort of.

We talked over the rest of the meal, about our families—who was doing what—he had more to tell me with all his brothers and their antics. He said his mother asked about me all the time. I asked him which one of the twins wanted to date my sister and he said, "They both do." We laughed.

When I looked at my watch it was almost ten o'clock. Wow, we'd been talking for almost four hours. "I really enjoyed this but I have an early meeting tomorrow morning," I said. I wanted to split the check. He insisted on paying it.

"Wait, I'll walk you to your car." He got up and pulled my chair out for me, left money for the bill on the table as we left.

We passed the bar and Dante asked the bartender if he needed to settle up when I noticed the bartender's nametag said Andy.

"Andy, you're friends with Julia, right? I'm her friend Brandy."

"Hey...yeah. Nice to meet you," Andy said. He stopped drying a glass and extended his hand across the bar to shake mine, then Dante's. "She can use all the friends she can get right now after this mess she's in."

"No kidding. She said she came here that night with

the guy. I don't believe she did it. Do you remember anything about them that night?" I asked. Dante's ears perked up.

"Well, the only thing sort of off was a girl came in and sat over there." He pointed to the corner table that was partially obstructed from the bar by a wall. "I think she could see the bar but they couldn't see her or they didn't pay attention to her. She came in through the open doors that lead out to the street over there, not through the bar door. Julia and the guy were already here. I didn't think much of it until she got up and left right after they did. That made me think she was following them."

Dante showed Andy his shield and said he would try to come back with some photos to see if Andy could ID her.

"Sure, just call first and make sure I'm here. I work all kinds of crazy hours. I hope I can help," Andy said.

Dante walked me to my car and I was excited, thinking of the hallway encounter, expecting him to kiss me. Instead, he took my keys, opened the door for me, thanked me for having dinner with him and said good night. As I drove home, I felt emotionally out of whack. At Julia's I didn't expect him to kiss me, and he did. Tonight, I wanted him to kiss me without all the family expectations dumped on us, and he didn't. Then, I saw headlights pull out behind me when I left the parking lot and figured, he was going to follow me and make sure I got home safely. Maybe he'd walk me to my door and kiss me good night then.

Chapter Eleven

I WAS BACK in my office setting up appointments with clients to review their communication firewalls when Jiff's number rang on my cell phone.

"Julia is going to be arrested and taken downtown for arraignment," he said before I could even say hello.

"What? What's going on?"

"I really wish I didn't have to tell you this. The police found a bloody dress they believe Julia wore the night they went out and a bronze statue exactly like the ones she has in the other guest rooms with the victim's bloody head matter all over it in a dumpster at the end of her street. They are sending both to forensics to run DNA and the prints," he said.

"Oh my God. What can I do to help?"

"I'll call you back when I get more info." He hung up and I sat there holding the phone.

This didn't make sense. I had to get to Julia and find out what happened. I called the bed and breakfast and Frank answered.

"Frank, stop crying. I know Julia didn't do it. What happened?" I asked.

He sniffled. "About ten cops showed up here an hour ago and said she was being arrested for the murder of Gervais St. Germain and started reading her rights. She looked so stunned she just barely got out telling me to call Jiff Heinkel's office, that's your friend's firm, right? His card is right here on the reception desk."

"What else did they say? Did they say where they were taking her?" It felt like an enormous hand was squeezing my chest.

"No, they hauled her off in handcuffs, and wouldn't say a thing to me. They would not answer one of my questions. I asked them where they were taking her but they just ignored me." He started crying again.

"Pull yourself together. Julia needs our help, your help right now. You have to stay there and take care of the guests and the hotel. How many guests are checked in?" I asked him.

"Five, I think, maybe four, no five. There are five guests here right now."

"Well, can you cook? Can you stay there and make them breakfast?" I asked him.

"I just clean, I don't know how to cook or serve food. I don't know how to check anyone in or out. I don't know how to run the credit card machine." He started crying again.

"Just write everything down, credit cards, peoples names, how long they stayed, we'll figure it out. I'll see if I can get our housekeeper to come help you. She's a good cook. Her name is Woozie… and Frank, just do your best in the meantime," I said, and hung up.

I called my parents house and sure enough Woozie, our housekeeper since I could remember, answered the phone. "The Alexander residence." She sounded like she was answering for the White House.

"Woozie, it's me and I need your help."

"Well, I don't see you or hear from you since you moved out. You don't call ole Woozie and tell me where you is living, what you is doing, who you is seeing and not seeing…nothing. Humph."

"I know, I'm sorry but I've kinda had my hands full with uh, life."

"Well, just so you know, I misses you and your daddy misses you. He can't stop talking about you. He's always saying, 'this is Brandy's favorite', or 'Brandy always takes seconds of that' when I make dinner. Your momma misses you too, even though she don't say it."

"Yeah, she misses me like a toothache. I'm sorry I haven't called you but I try to avoid my mother's house because of all the hoopla with me and Dante."

"Lawd, yes. Your momma can't stop talking about the mess you started by kissing that fella at the parade. Then, you up and move out so I don't hear or see you and I don't know nothing 'bout you and this new man except what your momma tells me. I know she goes and gets it all wrong. She won't tell me the truth what goes on wit you, just what she wants me to know. Now, all she can talk about is that friend of yours who done murdered some man dead in her hotel after she sleep wit him. How's your momma know that? She is calling her the Black Widow since her husband just died too. I saw that woman on the news. She's not black, why is your momma calling this woman black? I gotta hear all that from her. I don't hear from you to give me the real news. I don't think your momma has got all the facts."

"A black widow is a spider that kills its mate after they have sex."

"Really? Like a viper woman?"

"That would be a snake woman like Cleopatra. Look, I'll explain all that later. Woozie, I really need your help.

The police have arrested Julia and taken her in. There's only her...uh...houseman there who cleans and fixes things. There's no one to cook the breakfast for the guests. Can you go over there and help out until she gets released? I'll pay you if Julia can't."

"You want me to go help a murderess? A black widow spider woman, who kilt a man after she slept wit him?"

"She didn't kill anyone. I know Julia and you don't need to be afraid of her. This is a big mess." I started to plead when Woozie cut me off.

"Oh, I don't care if she gone and done it. Your momma thinks she killed him dead. This is gonna make her crazy enough to pitch a conniption fit when she hears I work there. She gonna think I know something she don't," she said, chuckling to herself. "Oh, yeah, I'll be there first thing in the morning. Early, right, and don't you go tell your momma I said that."

"Yes, the earlier the better, and I won't tell her if you don't. I mean, don't tell anyone, anything that you see or hear over there, except me."

"Oh, don't worry 'bout old Woozie. We been keeping secrets for each other since the night your daddy got drunk with his brother and named you. When they came home neither one of them could write their own name. I'm the one who wrote your name on that birth certificate. I know that and you know that. Your momma don't know and we gonna keep it that way. Woozie don't tell nobody nothing."

"I know my secrets are safe with you. I love you, Woozie. The guy, the cleaning man's name is Frank," I said, and then gave her the code to get in the back kitchen door.

Y Y Y

I WAS ABOUT to leave on my appointments when my cell phone rang and the police department's main number came up on caller I.D. It was Dante on the other end, in his official police—I'm not trying to win you back— voice, telling me that Julia was arrested and that I would most likely get called in for questioning.

"Are you going to question me," I asked him, "or another detective?" I wondered if Hanky Panky was finally going to realize her dream of interrogating me. She was probably out right now looking for the highest wattage light bulb to sit me under during questioning. She might get lucky and find a pair of brass knuckles on her shopping spree.

"I don't know. It won't be me." *Oh yeah, it was going to be Hanky Panky.* "I just wanted to give you a heads up. You might want to start to distance yourself from Julia. This has repercussions that could suck you in."

"Well, thanks for the warning, and oh, I wanted to thank you for following me home from the Napoleon House for my safety. You didn't have to do that."

"I didn't follow you home," he said, and hung up.

Y Y Y

I WAS JITTERY the rest of the day trying to stay focused. I had appointments to speak to clients who had complicated fraud problems and I needed to find solutions for them. Each time I was leaving a client's office, I was expecting a smiling Hanky Panky in a police car waiting at the door to haul me in for questioning. When there was no police car I watched my rear view mirror wondering if someone was following me, and why. I thought I was probably making something out of nothing.

At my last appointment of the day, I called on the largest liquor wholesale distributor in the city. I met with the CEO who outlined their problem with hackers trying to reroute deliveries. I reviewed this case and said I'd upgrade his firewall, run diagnostics and remote testing to see if he was still vulnerable.

"Thanks, Ms. Alexander."

"Please call me Brandy." I stood to leave and shook his hand.

"You know with your name you'd make a heck of a liquor salesperson." We both laughed. I picked up a bottle of Chianti he had on his desk and looked it over.

"Take it if you like red wine. My wife and I don't drink Chianti. A client, well I should say a friend, ordered it and gave me a bottle. We don't stock it. It was a special order."

"It looks like a bottle my friend's dad brought to my parents house when she announced she was getting married and asked me to stand," I said.

"Donnato Fortunata's daughter?" he asked.

"Yes. Small world. He's your customer?"

"I've known him and his family for years. I import that for him, usually a case at a time. He says it is the best Chianti from Italy, so he ordered several cases for his daughter's wedding."

"Yes, he brought a bottle of this to my parents' house. My dad loved it. New Orleans is great like that. If you talk to someone five minutes you will know someone they know. Now, I'm sure I'll see you at the wedding. It's going to be a big to do, this wedding and reception."

"Yes, Donnato is sparing no expense for his only daughter."

Ƴ   Ƴ   Ƴ

ALL AFTERNOON NOTHING happened and no one called me with an update. I finally called Jiff's office and his secretary told me he was working on Julia's 'situation' and he'd said to tell me he would call as soon as he could. She added that he would have Julia call me as soon as she was released.

When I heard from Jiff later that evening he told me he put me on the defendant's witness list and he said the prosecution would probably treat me as a hostile witness at trial since Julia called me right after the murder. We set up a time at his office so he could prep me to anticipate their questions which he felt would try to make me look like I helped her cover up evidence. I was more worried than ever, now that it was looking like Julia and her case were going to trial.

Julia was about to have a nervous breakdown by the time Jiff bonded her out late that evening. I went by the B&B after I stopped home to explain what I had done earlier since Woozie was there. I wanted to eyeball her and see how she was handling all this.

"Woozie is at your hotel because I asked her to come and take care of breakfast and help out," I said.

"Frank was here," she said absently. Her face was red and her eyes were puffy from crying.

"Yes, I know, but Frank can't cook. He told me so

and I thought Woozie could help him and fix breakfast," I said. "Woozie is very organized and Frank… well, Frank isn't. But, he's helpful and very distraught over your situation." She looked up at me for criticizing Frank. "Woozie was more than happy to do it." I added.

"Woozie? Happy to help me? I suppose that is a good idea in case I'm hauled out of here again. What I keep going over and over in my mind is I could go to jail for a murder I didn't commit and what is going to become of this place. Who do I have to run it? I'll never recover from this." She paused to blow her nose. "You wanna hear the best? More people are calling to make a reservation thinking it's haunted here because it used to be a funeral home. They ask how many murders have taken place here over the years and what ghost is actually doing the murders? Can you believe it?" she asked.

"You know you can't buy marketing like that. However, it might be a good idea not to mention to Woozie that people think this place is haunted. She didn't seem to mind the fact that someone was murdered here, but haunted and ghosts are another story with Wooz. Anyway, use the bump in business to help pay your attorney fees for your defense. This case might go on for awhile but it would be great for business if you got a reputation for having paranormal activity."

"What? You think people want to stay in a place that's haunted?" She blew her nose again.

I lowered my voice. "People drive all the way to St. Francisville to spend a night in plantations they claim have spirits roaming around in them. It's way out in the country with nothing to do except wait around to be spooked. But seriously, don't say the "h" word or the "g" word around Woozie, got it?"

"Oh, all right, I'll try to remember and I'll tell Frank not to say it's…" Julia only mouthed the word haunted.

I hesitated but then plunged in. "Did the police find your dress with the statue in the dumpster down the street? The way the room looked, it seemed all your clothes were off and hanging from the chandelier."

"I wore that dress in there but it didn't stay on long and I really didn't miss it when you or the police got here. I didn't notice the statue missing either. The statue is a knock off, not a real antique so it isn't worth much."

"That's not the point. This isn't an insurance claim. If you didn't put your dress back on to leave the room, what did you wear when you left?" Julia's answers were starting to confuse me. If I found flaws in her story, I could only imagine how the prosecutor would rake her over the coals.

"I didn't wear anything, I just got out of bed and went to shower. There was no one else registered here to see me. It's more or less like I told you. I did shower and dress before I called you. I woke up next to him and I never really looked at him before I got out of the bed, but now I realize he had to have been dead already. I showered thinking it would make me feel better. I thought I cut myself because I saw blood run off me in the shower. It didn't even occur to me it might not be mine. I told you, everything felt blurry, like a really bad hangover. I dressed, went down to make us some breakfast and dropped the tray like I said when I went back into the room and saw him dead. I checked to see if he had a pulse. That's when I called you. I knew he was dead. I think I was in the bed with him when he was killed. I just don't remember anything."

"OK, how did your dress and the bronze statue get into the dumpster?"

"I don't know. I didn't put them there and my dress was off when we got into bed. If he were killed next to me, I would have had to be wearing it to get that blood all over it. The last thing I do remember was him taking it off me when I walked in the door. It was off somewhere across the bedroom."

"No one is going to believe that after they hear you showered and dressed. It's going to sound like you tried to cover it up or get rid of evidence."

"Why would I have blood all over my hands if I wanted to look like I was covering it up. I would have picked up all my clothes and removed everything of mine out of the room, wouldn't I?"

She had a point. "What about the glasses and the wine bottle? Did you wash the glasses in the bathroom and leave them there?" I asked her.

"No, I thought they were where we left them."

"Where was that?" I asked her.

"I don't remember."

"Well, take a deep breath and try. This is very important," I said.

She thought a minute and said, "I remember he handed me a glass after opening the bottle, but I don't remember where I put my glass or if he took it from me."

"The glasses were in his bathroom when the police found them," I said.

"I don't remember if I washed or moved them and I didn't notice if the wine bottle was still here. Did the police find the wine bottle?" she asked.

"They found a wine bottle in the dumpster smashed

along with your dress and the statute they think is the murder weapon. The forensics' team is running tests to see if it's the missing wine bottle and whose fingerprints, besides yours and St. Germain's, are on it and if it contained the drug. I gotta tell you, this doesn't look good for you. You need to tell Jiff everything and hope he can run interference so some of this never comes out, but in all likelihood it will. You will need to brace yourself for the worst."

Chapter Twelve

JULIA WAS ARRESTED, a trial date was set for six months out, and things changed for me with Jiff and Dante.

Dante kept his distance since he was still on the case. I didn't see him or hear from him regarding Julia, the case, or for any other reason. He didn't contact me again after he phoned the day Julia was arraigned. One evening, when I stopped to visit my parents, I saw him starting to walk out of his parents' house next door. When he spotted my car, he went back inside. So much for his working to get me back. The trial could get continued and who knew how long this could drag on.

On the other hand, Jiff and I saw each other almost every day. We were going dancing at Rock 'n Bowl, or to hear a band we both liked. We went out with his friends and mine. We were getting to know each other. Jiff took me to his favorite place for donuts, which was a bakery in someone's garage on Verbena Street. They made the best tasting donuts in the world. The donut man wore an all white uniform complete with a paper military type hat and made them while you waited. The owner sat in a reclining lawn chair with a cigar box and took the money for your order. I don't think the New Orleans Health Department knew of or ever inspected this garage/bakery. If an inspector did come here, it was to order donuts.

We were doing normal things people do who like each other and date. He treated me like a princess. On

Sundays he would come pick me up and we'd take our dogs, Meaux Jeaux and Isabella, to the dog park or he would come by on his motorcycle and we'd ride to a festival somewhere. He bought me all custom BMW gear, a helmet, matching leather jacket and leather pants, gloves and all the necessary protection I needed for the road. It was wonderful to ride on his K 1600 BMW, leaning against his back with my arms wrapped around him. We went to the Ponchatoula Strawberry Festival, the Sauce Piquant Festival and sampled every way Cajuns made piquant. Sitting behind him on his motorcycle had us close and in physical contact, touching each other all day. When we took off our helmets he would use a finger and gently move an errant wisp of hair off my face. We enjoyed the food, the music and checked out the local antique shops. If I wanted to do something, he wanted to do it with me.

Jiff supported my rescue efforts, never complaining about how many dogs I had at my apartment, and always considered what I had to say regarding Julia's matter. He never dismissed me. Our bond was getting stronger and closer. I still wasn't sure if I was ready to cut the line on Dante, at least not yet, not until after the wedding or Julia's outcome, whichever came first. Jiff and I still had a lot to find out about each other and we were enjoying each other's company doing just that. He was the consummate gentleman in all things. He never pushed me or rushed me to become more romantically involved although I was thinking about it more and more.

Jiff's firm was working hard trying to find Violet Fornet to question her about Gervais St. Germain's murder. She was nowhere to be found. Jiff told me Ernest had interviewed the Pancake Paddy manager who said Violet hadn't shown up for work in a couple of weeks. Yes, they remembered hearing about the murder up the street, but no one could remember the last time they saw Violet, at work or anywhere. She and the other servers worked hours that could only be figured out by the schedulers who managed flight crews for airlines. Sometimes she worked the 3:00 a.m. until 11:00 a.m. shift, or she worked lunches 10:00 a.m. until 2:00 p.m., or sometimes she worked split shifts but only if someone would split the shifts with her. Sometimes she didn't show up even if she was on the schedule. What he did find out was that Violet had another guy friend she would see whenever she broke up with Gervais. The servers at Pancake Paddy said this guy would sit at the counter when Violet worked and wait for her to get off. No, they didn't know his name and Violet didn't seem overly interested in him. They said she treated him more platonically and he always paid cash. They didn't remember much about him but she never claimed to have dated anyone other than Gervais.

Julia signed a statement allowing Jiff and his firm to share information with me they received or obtained regarding her case. Julia's parents were dead, her ex-husband was dead and she hadn't spoken with her brother in years. In fact, she had no idea where he lived or how to find him. She thought a friendly pair of eyes who believed she was innocent would help.

Then, an odd thing happened.

"Brandy, did Jiff or that investigator call you?" asked Julia in lieu of a hello, when I answered my phone.

"No, why?"

or what she has to do with her disappearance other than the Gervais St. Germain connection. There's nothing we know connecting Julia to Violet, but I want to see what the police think the connection is."

"Be careful with her, Jiff. She's really fragile right now, and I don't trust her not to blurt out something stupid like, 'maybe I did it," I said.

"I'm not going to let her say a word."

I followed Jiff and Julia downtown to the police complex located at 715 South Broad Street corner of Tulane Avenue. This was my second visit here in less than a month. The first time was when they arrested Julia and threw her in Central Lockup. Once I parked and found the correct room in the maze of corridors inside, I had to wait on a very uncomfortable metal bench in a hallway while they questioned Julia.

When they were finished, I agreed to meet both Jiff and Julia back at the guest house for the debriefing. I stopped at a ladies' room and when I came out, Dante was waiting for me.

"This is getting worse for Julia, and you need to watch yourself or you will be tied to this mess with her," he said.

"Oh, hello Dante, long time no speak," I mouthed off. "Tell Hanky I'm sorry I missed her. I see you two are still partners."

"I see you're still dating Jiff," he responded, the vein in his head pumping.

"Oh, another intimate conversation with you here, in the middle of police headquarters."

"I can't be contacting you or talking with you while I'm working this case. You're too involved and you need to be careful." That vein was working overtime.

"We could act like adults." He had turned on his heel, left me standing and talking to myself.

Y Y Y

BACK AT JULIA'S, Jiff waited for me before rehashing what had happened. Jiff thought the questions were a fishing expedition. He said Dante conducted the interview and asked the questions. At one point, Hanky got up, seemed furious about something and left the room.

"She always seems furious about something," I said.

Jiff read the questions Dante asked from his notes:

Did you know Violet Fornet?
No.
Did you know she was from Chicago?
No.
Did you know Gervais St. Germain was her boyfriend?
No.

Dante told them Violet's family had called the New Orleans Police Department from Chicago to file a missing persons report because she had not called home for over two weeks, highly irregular for her. The last call she made home was on the night of or the night after the St. Germain murder according to the date Violet's dad said he remembered last speaking with her. The police figured Julia knew Violet since she knew St. Germain.

Then the clincher.

Was Julia jealous of Violet for planning a wedding

with Gervais, and did she know Violet was pregnant
with his child?

This topped them all. Now, the police thought Julia was the third person in a love triangle, which gave them the big motive they had been looking for.

"I thought we were home free," Jiff said. "Then, Dante asked Julia again if she knew or ever met Violet Fornet. When Julia answered no, Dante pulled out a photo of Violet to show Julia. When Julia looked at the photo closely she realized, and blurted out, that Violet was the person who delivered coffee and lunches she ordered from Pancake Paddy when she was restoring the bed and breakfast. So, now the police had confirmation that Julia did know both Gervais and Violet." Jiff said this was the motive they needed to keep Julia as their number one suspect.

"Well, for that matter, I could know Violet. You know how it is here; sooner or later you seem to bump into everyone or cross paths. New Orleans is a very small, big city," I said.

"Yeah, but Violet went in and out of that bed and breakfast. The police now have proven Julia did know her and they believe she lied to them about that. It's their idea of a motive even if it's wrong. They can put Julia and Violet together and assume they talked, got to know each other when the deliveries were made."

It didn't help that the police didn't discover Violet was missing. They might have, had they interviewed her place of employment. Only they didn't look into Violet or her place of employment or anything to do with her relationship with Gervais St. Germain. They didn't follow up on her until the family filed the missing person report. Knowing that the path of least resistance was an attractive route, the police made their way back to Julia to tie her relationship with the former boyfriend to this missing woman as a crime of passion.

"I have a question." I asked Jiff, exasperated for Julia, "Since the two people involved in this so far both were slipped roofies, how is this a crime of passion? It seems to me like a crime of passing out."

"The police believe it's a lover's triangle and Julia killed him in bed when she found out about the wedding, the baby, all of it. The police just added charges of drugs and are looking at Julia for the possible murder of Violet Fornet since no one can find her. You might want to go upstairs and talk to Julia. She was a nervous wreck after she saw that photo of Violet and I think she's lying down," Jiff said.

"I can't believe Julia didn't recognize her from what's plastered on TV," I said.

"No one would. The photo of Violet they showed Julia was from a State ID the police pulled up from Chicago," Jiff said.

"It probably looks more like the waitress who delivered the coffee here than the glamour shots they are posting on TV," I said.

"Julia is now connected to Violet and St. Germain. The police have proof she knew them both. This case just got harder. What St. Germain promised or knew about Violet and her pregnancy needs to be better documented. He's the common denominator." Jiff was reading the transcript from the questioning. He made a call into his office and spoke to Ernest Devereaux, advising him to pull out all the stops to locate Violet or her last known whereabouts. "Forget that the police are even investigating, act like they're not. Call in Michelle to help you run down leads, or for anything you need, anything at all. Michelle has contacts with the band and maybe she can get some fast answers. I think the police dropped the ball on this one, so do your thing. We need to find out everything we can about this woman and find her before they do. I want cameras rolling when we find her and I want it to be our side of the story being told." Jiff hung up and looked at me. "I don't mean to slam the police or your friend, but we can't let this slide until something pops up. We need to make it pop up."

"Maybe Dante dropped the ball, maybe he didn't. Could he be holding back evidence?" Part of me didn't want Dante to look bad at his job, as angry as I was with him, I didn't want anything bad to happen to him unless I was the one to make it happen. Call it a female thing, I wanted to run him over with an eighteen-wheeler, back up over him and make sure he saw it was me driving. That was the kind of bad I wanted to make happen to Dante.

"They can withhold evidence until discovery," Jiff answered. "Ernest should have something soon. We need to find Violet."

The more I went over those questions in my mind, the more I started to think maybe Dante gave up more than he got in that interview. It could be why Hanky stormed out of there.

🍸 🍸 🍸

JIFF CALLED IN a favor from a friend at NOPD who got hold of the missing person report on Violet Fornet and relayed what he learned. Not hearing from Violet set off the Fornets' worry alarm thinking something terrible had happened to her. They called the New Orleans Police to report her missing when they couldn't reach her boyfriend, Gervais St. Germain. That was when they discovered, or rather, were told by the police, that Gervais St. Germain had been murdered. The family told the police they knew it must be connected to Violet's disappearance because their daughter and Gervais were going to be married. The family also told the police they had been sending money to Violet for her wedding plans.

Boy, did she have her family snowed. Her parents seemed like nice people who believed their daughter was making a life for herself here, not drugging it up with some weirdo, killing peoples' pets and stalking a guitar player. They were going to be shocked when this all came out.

Over the next two weeks Violet's disappearance gained momentum in the press. The family flew in from Chicago and held candlelight vigils up and down the street where she was last seen leaving the bar with her friend. The family spent money and paid for full-page ads in the local newspapers offering a reward for information leading to her whereabouts. They printed signs and posted them up and down where she worked and the entire street by the bar where they held the vigils. Signs littered a square mile along the neutral grounds—the grassy space between streets otherwise known as the median in other parts of the world—and every major intersection with a very flattering photo of Violet from the pre-cocaine snorting period of her life. The local news media came out to film one nightly vigil and did a spot on the evening news with the family holding their family pet, crying and asking for everyone to help find Violet. I thought I'd hide that pet if I were them. If Violet was found, and if what I'd learned about her was true, they might be crying over Fido. They made her sound like a saint, St. Violet, not the pet-murdering, hustling, cocaine addict I believed she was.

As Violet's story unfolded daily in the papers and on the nightly news, so did Julia's apparent involvement with Gervais St. Germain as the other woman. The family believed—and the news ate it up—that Gervais was planning to marry dear Violet and start their family. Violet had told her parents she thought she was pregnant and that she and Gervais were beginning to plan their wedding. All she needed was ten thousand dollars for deposits on a church, reception hall, band and caterer, oh yes, and the OB-GYN. She was going to need tests done to make sure her baby had good medical prenatal care. Her parents, excited over the idea of a grandchild and Violet getting married, sent the money.

After a day of listening to the news pound on about Violet, Jiff called in the afternoon and invited me to dinner after work. He asked me to meet him at his office in Canal Place. I told him I'd be happy to. He and I had been so focused on Julia and her trial that we hadn't been spending as much time together the last two weeks. When we did see each other it was about Julia. I missed him. I missed how much attention he paid to me. Jiff made me feel like I was the only girl on the planet when I was with him.

It was Wednesday, a few minutes before 5:00 p.m. and I was preparing to leave my office when the receptionist buzzed me and said I had a delivery. I packed up for the day and when I got to her desk there were a dozen red roses waiting for me.

"Baby, dat man who sent dem roses, and dey are beautiful, loves you, sugar," Miss Ella said in her ninth ward accent which dropped the "g" on ing and changed all words that started with a "th" to "d." She spoke New Orleansese. She greeted all employees, all the time adding endearments of darling, baby or sugar to the beginning and ending of every sentence.

I opened the envelope addressed to me and the card said; *I've made a reservation at the most romantic restaurant in New Orleans for us tonight. I can't wait to see you and spend an evening alone together. Love, Jiff.*

The *Love, Jiff* surprised me for a second and then it didn't. He was not shy about how he felt about me and I liked it. I was floating on air when I left my office on Poydras Street in the One Shell Square Building and walked up St. Charles to Canal Street. When I got to that corner I stopped to window shop at Rubenstein's—a high-end clothing store for men and women. It looked as if Jiff was their poster boy for this place. The suits he wore all looked like they came from here. Dante dressed on a cop's salary and he always looked great in whatever he wore even though his approach to clothes was a whole lot different than Jiff's. Dante's mother used to buy all her boys' suits off the rack at Sears because she said she could throw them in the washing machine and get the stains out. I was thinking she saved a lot of money on dry cleaning since her five boys were always rough housing even when they were dressed up when I felt someone walk up close behind me. I looked up in the window reflection to see it was Little Tony.

Without turning around I said, "Fancy meeting you here. You shop at Rubenstein's?" Even if Little Tony did shop at this haberdashery he would make whatever he wore look like it belonged on a hit man.

"Naw, who wants to be trussed up like a turkey at Thanksgiving in one of those suits all day? I'm more of a casual guy," he said.

"So, why are you here?" I asked him and turned to face him. He was wearing the wise guy uniform of black shirt, black tie and black jacket. "You look hot in that." I realized I made a poor choice of words immediately.

"Yeah? I think you look pretty hot yourself. Why don't you and I go get a drink somewhere?" He was back doing the pimp-bouncing thing with his head on every word.

"Thanks for the invite, but I'm on my way to a meeting in Canal Place," I said tapping my watch with a finger.

"Well, why don't I wait for you and we go get a drink after your meeting," he said.

Something about the way Little Tony was pushing his agenda having just popped up downtown in the business district gave me crawly skin. My gut was saying not to trust him or tell him exactly what my plans were. "Thanks anyway, but maybe some other time because this could go on for hours and I have no idea when it will end." I looked at my watch and said, "Oh gosh, I'm going to be late…see you at the wedding." I hurried away from him before he could come up with some other lame brain idea.

Jiff's office was on the top floor and I arrived about 5:30 and found him talking with Ernest in his corner office, the one with the spectacular view of the curves in the Mississippi River. I could sit there for hours and watch freighters or cruise ships sail by or the Algiers Ferry fight the Mississippi River currents to maneuver turns or approach the docks.

"Hey, Brandy." He waved me in. "Ernest has uncovered more info on Violet over the last twenty-four hours," Jiff said when he spotted me outside his office.

I greeted them both as Jiff came around from behind his desk and put a hand on each shoulder and we exchanged a loving kiss, a lot more than a peck on the cheek. Ernest stood up when he saw me and we gave each other a hello kiss on the cheek. The New Orleans custom of kissing hello or goodbye on the cheek with someone is indicative of how comfortable friends and business associates are with you. If you don't know them or have just met, then you just shake hands. Jiff ushered both of us to a round table off to one end of his spacious corner office where he pulled a chair for me to sit after he helped me off with my suit jacket and hung it on the coat rack in the corner. Ernest and Jiff took seats and Ernest pulled out his notebook.

Jiff brought me up to speed on their findings, "Ernest verified the information on the missing persons report that Violet hadn't called home in over two weeks. He pulled her cell records and the family phones to see when she stopped calling. He cross-referenced the names and Violet's calls stopped about eighteen days ago. She was the only child and had lived with her family in Chicago until she came to New Orleans to visit during Jazz Fest over a year ago, fell in love with Gervais, the city and the never ending party and decided to stay. She met Gervais playing in a bar one night. Initially, she moved in with St. Germain who shared an apartment with a roommate while he was in New Orleans playing music. Six months of the year he usually travelled with the band all up and down the river playing at college frat house parties or honky tonks. Violet got a job as a Fabulous Flipper— what they called the servers, at Pancake Paddy and called home regularly, weekly, sometimes twice a week, asking for money."

Ernest said, "I verified this by obtaining Violet's bank account and the sums that were regularly transferred into it. Large sums of money were deposited into the account in Chicago while only withdrawals were made by Violet here in New Orleans. It was always cash. There were no withdrawals or checks drawn to indicate she ever paid rent or a light bill. No checks were ever written for a deposit on anything remotely associated with a wedding, i.e. caterer, dress, church, restaurant…nothing."

Jiff said, "Michelle, you remember our other investigator, was told by the wives and girlfriends of the band members who lived in the New Orleans area that Violet would give them a sob story asking to stay with them a few days and that would turn into weeks, then months, or until they had enough and told her she had to find another place. She never rented or had her own place and she wasn't selective where she crashed. She'd go home with anyone who offered her a place for the night, only they didn't realize it was going to be until they kicked her out."

Ernest said, "I discovered the names of other people

Violet stayed with and went to interview them. All the people told me variations of the same story. They all said they felt sorry for her at first because she was pitiful, moved here for love, then the guy cheated on her, or this was the story Violet told them. They gave her the boot when some sleazy guy started hanging round. They figured he was supplying her with drugs, then they wanted both gone so they would ask her to leave."

Ernest went on, "At one couple's apartment I noticed an empty dog bed with a photo of the dog in it. I asked the lady, 'I'm sorry, did you lose your pet?' She said, yes, her little dog, Pork Chop, was poisoned. She started to cry asking why would someone do that to her sweet little dog? When I asked her if it happened when Violet was staying with them, a look of shock came over her face. Then she said, 'If she poisoned my dog, I'll track her down and kill her myself.'"

Ernest reported he spoke to the servers where she worked and they told him that Violet made good tips because her customers felt sorry for her and her sad stories. The other servers told him Violet wasn't a good co-worker since she made a habit of not showing up and leaving them to cover her shifts even when she said she always needed money. Ernest said two of her co-workers told him they thought she had a drug problem due to her inability to maintain a regular schedule. One of servers told Ernest the guy who was interested in Violet came by when Violet wasn't working and offered her a twenty-dollar bill to make a call to the new bed and breakfast up the street and ask if some guy had checked in. She remembered it being the day Gervais was killed and Violet had not shown up for work.

The Pancake Paddy manager also got a sob story and felt sorry for her, telling Ernest she thought Violet had a bum musician for a boyfriend but she wouldn't commit to thinking Violet did drugs. She let Violet work when she showed up since the counter was always short handed. Ernest said she told him, "Look around, this isn't Commander's Palace."

Ernest said, "I asked to see Violet's timecards for the hours she worked so I could come up with a timeline of where she was and where she wasn't. The manager told me she didn't use timecards, only that she kept a running tally of hours worked on a sheet of paper in her office. She didn't write down dates, or times, just hours worked. She would write out their checks on payday, and then throw away the piece of paper. That's how she did her payroll."

I asked, "Ernest, did the manager say if she remembered the last day Violet showed up?"

"That was weeks ago and all the papers with their dates and times worked were long gone. The manager did say a guy came by a few times after Violet was a definite no show before he stopped coming to look for her," he answered.

No one seemed to know the name of the guy but they all described him the same—a sleaze. Big help, what drug dealer wasn't a sleaze?

Pitiful little Violet had a good hustle to advance her drug problem and didn't mind taking advantage of just about anyone to keep it going. When Gervais went on the road with the band to get away from Violet, the roommate kicked her out. He told Ernest that Gervais and Violet were on again, off again boyfriend and girlfriend as long as there was free flowing cocaine. They had that in common and it was the way she controlled him. When he started to stray she'd show up with the fun and he'd follow her anywhere until it ran out and she had to supply more. Thus, the calls home for money.

Ernest told us he tracked down the girlfriend who was the last person seen with Violet late on the very night of the murder. The bar, which on the news looked like The Ritz, was a dive bar out by the lake. It wasn't even air-conditioned.

"The bartender told me he didn't remember either of the two women who were there drinking on the last night Violet was seen alive. He finally had his memory jogged when I slapped down a hundred dollar bill for the name of the friend." Ernest looked at Jiff and said, "Sorry boss, cost of doing business." He went on, "When I went to the home of this friend, she said she would tell me what she knew but she wished to remain anonymous. She didn't want to be on the news or called into court. Violet asked this friend to use her cell phone that night to get a money transfer from her folks in order to continue drinking."

Ernest said, "I asked this friend, why was Violet drinking if she was pregnant? The friend looked surprised and told me, if she was pregnant it was news to her. She knew Violet could scam her folks for money but she didn't think she'd take it that far."

Ernest said, "I asked her if she remembered exactly what night this was? She told me it was on her cell phone in the history and showed me the call Violet made to Chicago. It was the morning of the St. Germain murder. The time was 1:00 a.m. and according to Julia, she and Gervais didn't get back to the bed and breakfast from their drinks in the French Quarter until 1:30 a.m. or

2 a.m. They left Napoleon House around midnight which Andy confirmed and she said they walked around for a while before they caught a taxi."

"So what do you think happened that night to make Violet want to go drinking?" I asked.

"This friend said Violet was upset when she met her at the bar. Violet told her she had seen Gervais' earlier that day and Gervais had said he loved her. He also told Violet where he was staying but didn't ask her to stay with him. When she went to surprise him at the bed and breakfast, she saw him leaving the hotel with a woman. Violet thought he had checked in with her so she followed them. We know the bartender saw Violet leave after St. Germain and Julia left."

"What time does the coroner put the time of death?" Jiff asked flipping through the file looking for the report.

"I want to say it was between 1:00 a.m. and 3:00 a.m." I said.

"Yes, you're right. Here it is." He read the report, and then passed it to me.

"Violet's friend said they left the bar at 4:30 a.m. and she was pretty lit up," said Ernest.

"Did you find out how much they had to drink?" I asked.

"I had to pull it out of the friend because she didn't want to get the bartender in trouble. He should have cut Violet off or taken her keys away, but the friend told the bartender she would take care of Violet," Ernest said.

"So, how many?" Jiff asked.

"Well, the bill was $93.00. She was doing shots of tequila and the friend had two cosmos," said Ernest.

"So, at top shelf tequila prices, that would be...." I

said, trying to calculate in my head.

"So, she had about seven or eight shots if your drinks were $8-10 each. Sound about right?" Jiff said.

"Yep, that's what the friend said Violet ordered. She told her friend, this time it's really over, saying that's what Gervais liked, top shelf liquor and she was drinking to erase his memory," said Ernest. "Yeah, that's what the friend said they paid for and a couple of guys sent shots down to Violet earlier. Violet also told her she did a little coke with the bartender while she waited for her. With all that, and the drinks, she had to be nuclear. I don't know how she could walk, let alone drive," said Ernest.

"Do you think one of those guys who sent the drinks waited for her?" I asked.

"I don't know, but I don't think so. The friend said those guys who bought her shots left about 2:00 a.m.," Ernest read from his notes.

"When did the friend last see Violet that night? Did Violet go home with her?" asked Jiff.

"Well, she said Violet was having trouble walking and was slurring her words so she offered to take her home even though she thought she would never get rid of her. Violet told her she was going to catch a few winks in her car first before she tried to drive and the girl never pressed it."

"What time was this? What time did they leave the bar?" asked Jiff.

"The friend said they walked out around 4:30 a.m. and the bartender confirms them leaving at 4:30 a.m. when he closed out their tab."

"So, Violet followed Gervais with Julia to the Napoleon House and leaves when they leave at midnight. She goes to meet her friend at the bar for 1:00 a.m. the same time Gervais and Julia are walking around the French Quarter and stays there during the timeframe he's supposed to have been killed at Julia's?" Jiff asked.

Ernest recapped, "Yes, given that timeline. Violet was in that bar with her friend and given the drinks and drugs her friend said she was having, I doubt she could have masterminded this crime at the spur of the moment and pulled it off. She would have had to slip out of the bar, drive to the bed and breakfast, climb a tree, open a window, slip in and bash St. Germain in the head with enough force to kill him with one blow and slip out, unnoticed. Also, she'd have to think fast enough to take the dress, statue, and maybe the wine bottle with her and toss them in a dumpster up the street? This scenario figures Violet thought it through to frame Julia along the way."

"Well, there goes using Violet to create reasonable doubt for Julia," Jiff said.

"I gave Violet's friend my card and told her we needed to find Violet. I asked her to please contact me if she hears from her. I hope she turns up, safe, no matter what her situation is," Ernest said.

"In New Orleans, there's a fine line between the good times and the crimes," Jiff said.

Chapter Thirteen

OUR MEETING ENDED and when we were alone in his office I thanked him for the roses and gave him a long, slow kiss that conveyed my appreciation.

"Wow, I guess you liked them. I was afraid you didn't get them before you left for the day," he said.

"Well, I didn't want to say anything in front of Ernest. I thought you might want to keep that personal."

"I don't care who knows how I feel about you. I called that order for the flowers in myself, just so you know. I didn't have my secretary do it," he said smiling and very proud of himself.

"So the most romantic restaurant in New Orleans?" I asked.

"Have you been to Feelings?" Jiff asked.

"No, I haven't been there and it sounds perfect."

"Great. I made us a reservation," he said with that smile that made my butterflies have butterflies. He helped me into my suit jacket. Jiff's manners would rival that of a British Royal. I felt like a Princess in his company. If there was a red carpet needed, he'd roll it out for me, I'm sure. He picked up his suit jacket off the coat stand behind the door of his office and swung it over his shoulder holding it with one finger. He looked like a model on the cover of GQ Magazine. He stepped forward and opened every door for me all the way out of the building.

He hailed us a pedicab outside of the Canal Place

Towers. We squeezed in next to each other while our cyclist peddled through the French Quarter down Decatur Street, past Jackson Square, Café du Monde and the French Market, all-alive in the evening with tourists and fun-loving locals. Jiff instructed the cabbie to take St. Peter Street to Esplanade Avenue as our route. This boulevard was beautiful in the early evening. While the driver pedaled taking us to our destination we travelled less hurried than those around us in motorized vehicles and enjoyed the peaceful pace of the pedicab.

"This is the perfect way for us to slow down our day," I said. We rode holding hands under a canopy of oak trees lined with blooming azaleas along one of the languid avenues framing the French Quarter. The speed we travelled reminded me of a time when ladies sashayed by these glorious mansions along this historic boulevard. I imagined then as I was seeing now, people walking their dogs, chatting to one another and stepping out to dinner from these mansions, once grand homes now turned guest houses. Times changed and certainly fashions had as well, but people still did the same things now as they did then in the same footsteps for the last hundred years here. The breeze was delightful as our human powered transportation pedaled faster and faster.

"Please, take your time," Jiff said to our driver while looking at me and moving a wisp of my hair off my face with his finger. He kissed me and people in passing cars honked their approval. The pedicab driver slowed down.

Our ride was over much too soon when our driver deposited us at Feelings Cafe on Chartres Street at the corner of Franklin. Jiff held my hand as I stepped off the pedicab and walked right into his arms as the driver pedaled away.

"I could do this every night with you," he said as we stood face to face with our arms around each other's waists. "Let's go have a drink and you can tell me about your day."

This restaurant sits in the original 'suburb' of New Orleans, just outside of the French Quarter, off the beaten path in Faubourg Marigny. The unhurried trip down Esplanade carried forward as we entered Feelings Café. Once a plantation home, the building had been totally restored to the beautiful lady she once was. Our host greeted us in the entryway of exposed brick walls with its grand curving staircase. He told us our table was waiting.

Jiff told the host, "We would first like to sit on the patio and have a cocktail, and then be moved to our table. Is that OK with you?" He asked me and I nodded.

"Of course," the host smiled "Right this way." He escorted us to a bistro table for two in the patio area steps from the bar and the coziest place next to a murmuring fountain. The bar was uniquely interesting in that it was home to some original Elvis and Marilyn Monroe memorabilia displayed in the most tasteful of ways. My parents had taken us on a family vacation to Graceland as kids. My mother, a big Elvis fan, cried at the gravesite out back. All I remember about that trip was that Elvis made tacky shag a home style much like traditional or colonial. In here, his memory and Marilyn's was—well—classy.

Our host and bartender spoke in soft voices keeping the ambience intimate. Even with couples seated at tables near us, voices whispering to each other made us feel we had the place to ourselves, having stepped into the past for a delightful evening. I ordered an Old Fashioned and Jiff asked if they made a good Brandy Alexander. He asked the waiter if he knew the cocktail was named after a beautiful woman. The waiter suspected it was a trick question while we smiled at each other at the inside joke.

When the waiter left with the drink order I said, "Thanks, you make me feel beautiful."

"That's because you are, and I admire the rescue work you do." He moved his chair closer to mine putting his arm around the back of my chair.

I felt my face getting hot from the compliments I didn't know how to graciously receive. I came from a family who only commented when you did something wrong, looked bad in what you were wearing or suggested you wear less makeup so you wouldn't look like a streetwalker leaving to go out. Compliments were non-existent at my house. I did not know how to receive one and it felt awkward. I might have to work on getting used to this. My family also thought rescue work was just about bringing home another smelly, abandoned dog nobody else wanted. Technically, this was true, and while my dad saw the point of rescue he was very careful not to make his opinion too clear in front of my mother.

We enjoyed our cocktails in an unhurried, civilized manner. We lingered awhile over our drinks, holding hands, Jiff pushing that errant wisp of hair out of my face again. He had me laughing at childhood stories he told about his brothers and the tricks they played on each other. He managed to slip into the conversation that he had told his parents about me.

Our host appeared as if reading our minds when we were ready to move to our table.

It was also quiet in the main dining room with a modest crowd all talking nose to nose. We were seated in a corner near French doors that opened to the street. We told the waiter we were in no particular hurry for our meal so he left the menus. Jiff asked to see the wine list and he returned a few minutes later with it and also an appetizer of Oysters En Brochette saying it was on the house and to take as much time as we needed. He'd check on us in a few minutes.

"Do you come here a lot?" I asked. "They seem to know you."

"My parents come here with my family often. My mother loves this place and plans, at a minimum, weekly dinners for her and my dad here, and a private party for every anniversary, every birthday or event—even for her adult children—here. I'm sure they recognized my name since my mother makes a lot of reservations. Parties of more than four people are held in the upstairs private room where my rowdy family is usually sequestered. It keeps the bar and dining room intimate, so other diners do not have to endure our liquored up voices slurring or singing 'Happy Birthday'," he smiled.

I didn't want to tell him our family dinners brought to mind the year I was eight and my sister was five years old and my dad gave my mother the electric carving knife—something he wanted—as a Christmas gift. She was disappointed, to say the least, since she had dropped a million hints for diamond earrings. To let him know the level of her disappointment she swore she'd cut his heart out with said knife. Both my sister and I shudder, even now, when we recall that Christmas dinner with all our relatives. My dad uses that electric carving knife every holiday so it's unlikely that memory will ever fade since it's revisited yearly.

"I want you to know you are the first date I've ever brought here."

"Why, Mr. Heinkel, I think you're flirting with me," I said in my most charming southern drawl.

"I am, and I want you to know I think about you all the time," he said as he picked up an oyster wrapped in bacon with his fork and fed it to me.

"Wow, these are to die for," I said after tasting one.

"I'm glad you like them. They are my mother's favorite and she orders them for all our dinner parties," he said. "She swears the oysters keep the magic alive in their marriage," he added. He took one of my hands in his across the table. He touched all the rings I was wearing and asked me why I wore each one. He asked about my childhood and since I wanted to keep the relationship alive, I didn't tell him much. He asked how I knew Julia. Julia and I had met when we both worked at the Telecom Company. I left out that when she was laid off she went to work in the French Quarter as an exotic dancer, more accurately a pole dancer. I could also feel he was going to quiz me on my relationship with Dante and I definitely didn't want to go there.

The maître d' appeared at our table so suddenly we stopped our discussion.

"I don't mean to interrupt your conversation but you two are the most romantic couple in the room. I would like to send you a bottle of champagne compliments of the house. Please advise your waiter when you are ready after you finish your cocktails," he said.

Jiff thanked him and we looked at each other when he

left. The waiter appeared as if summoned telepathically with the ice bucket and popped the cork. He poured the golden hue of bubbles in two flutes. Jiff and I toasted to a lovely evening in spite of the conversation. It's hard not to smile at a handsome man across the table from you who hangs onto your every word while drinking expensive champagne. Jiff's face was easy to look at and his dimples simply added to the boyish charm. But it was his jet black eyes that pierced my soul. It was that intensity, along with him looking like James Bond in the tuxedo he was wearing, that made me walk out into the street and kiss him at a Mardi Gras parade even though I had never met him. The kiss we shared had sent a lightning bolt into my world and woke up my sleeping hormones. When he whispered to meet him at the end of the parade, I did. Of course he was shot at, taken to Charity Hospital and then we were both kidnapped, but all relationships have their challenges. It was working fine now.

"This is very nice champagne," I said after the waiter left and I saw the name on the bottle.

"It's my mother's favorite," Jiff said.

I wondered if his mother was sitting somewhere in the restaurant watching us. It almost felt like she was there having dinner and I waited for the surprise appearance asking to join her at her table. My worries were for naught.

Even in this romantic setting, our thoughts quickly returned to all the trouble with Julia. Discussion turned to all we'd learned. We recounted what we knew and didn't know:

- Julia knew Gervais in the biblical sense, and knew

Violet from delivering coffee and food from Pancake Paddy.

- We still didn't know who roofied Julia and Gervais. This was the biggest question along with, where was Violet?

- After an extensive police search, the wine bottle Julia said was in the room wasn't found anywhere in the hotel. If we could get prints off the bottle from the dumpster, assuming it was the wine bottle from the room, we might get a line on a credible suspect.

- Someone must have given the wine to Gervais spiked and he didn't know it. We thought it unlikely he knowingly did it to himself but stranger things have been known to happen. His blood alcohol levels may have contributed to spiking his own glass by accident. He didn't have any history with Rohypnol according to the band but there's always a first time. Violet had experience with Rohypnol and pets, so we suspected her of spiking the wine and giving it to Gervais. That would explain why he drank it, but now Violet was missing and St. Germain was dead so we couldn't ask them.

- The wine bottle in the dumpster was, for all we knew, just a wine bottle and not the one from the room. Jiff was still waiting on the report from the police department to verify whether or not it was the bottle from the room and if there were traces of Rohypnol on the glass recovered. It was a long shot, but we hoped a fingerprint other than Julia's or St. Germain's was on it too.

"How much Rohypnol has to be in a glass or how much of the glass do you have to partake to have the desired effect?" I asked as I took a sip of my champagne.

"Very little. One milligram in a glass would do the trick. Just sipping some from that flute of champagne you're drinking would have the desired effect," he said.

"I wouldn't have to drink the whole glass?" I asked, surprised at the minuscule amount needed to render someone incapable of moving or defending themselves.

"No, but the more you drink the longer the effect it has is what I was told by Ernest. He's the expert right now on roofies. I'll have to be by the time we go to trial," Jiff said. When he noticed a slight panic look start to cross my face, he changed his comment to, "if we go to trial. Don't worry about that now."

Violet went missing the same night Gervais was killed. What happened that day to cause the orbits of Julia, Violet and Gervais to collide? Julia couldn't be in two places at the same time drugged on roofies and neither could Violet, given the timeline or as intoxicated as the bartender and her friend made her out to be.

My theory had a nagging flaw that kept me coming back to the open window. At first I'd thought Violet followed Gervais and seeing him with someone else in a bed & breakfast, while she was sleeping in her car could have pushed her over the edge. That was the night she was last seen. Maybe she killed Gervais then took off back to Chicago. As much as I wanted the killer to be Violet, this meant she would have had to enter their room shortly after they were in it—around midnight—so she could have gotten to the bar to meet her friend. My theory had two flaws. One was St. Germain's time of death. It was very unlikely the Coroner, who had been the Coroner for umpteen years, had the time wrong. The second was someone had to be pretty strong to climb that tree and wait there until the time was right. That person might have waited a couple of hours and Violet was in the bar all that time.

Jiff's theory was Violet manipulated Gervais with cocaine. She had a habit, she had a supplier and a constant money source. Jiff doubted she would kill him. Why would she murder her future husband? She wanted Gervais to marry her, or so she told her family. She had gone back and forth before, so he thought after her hangover, she would go back with him again.

He agreed, this left a third person who had to have killed St. Germain and tried to frame Julia, but who and why?

"Hmmm, the plot thickens," Jiff mimicked in a Sherlock Holmes quip as he topped off our champagne glasses.

Michelle, Jiff's other investigator, had reported to him that the members of the band close to St. Germain swore Gervais didn't plan on marrying Violet. They did weigh in on the pregnancy saying "maybe a baby" since she went back and forth with Gervais on a regular basis, but Gervais never mentioned any paternal problems or obligations.

"Here's another fly in the ointment," Jiff said. "Michelle's report also said that Maurice had had enough of Gervais' drug use and had a lead guitar player lined up to play with them for Jazz Fest since St. Germain was often a no show for gigs or arrived wasted when he did show up. Maurice had already contracted his replacement for Jazz Fest and hadn't told Gervais yet."

"That must have been the guy we saw tuning up. I wonder why Maurice didn't mention this when we first spoke with him. Maurice had to know Gervais was supposed to be staying at Julia's B&B with them, or did he?" I said.

"One of the band members told Michele they were surprised when they heard Gervais was in New Orleans since he had not contacted them in a couple of months. If he thought he could waltz in and have his spot back whenever he wanted it, this might have caused a fight within the band. Maybe several band members were worried he'd cause problems once he found out he was being replaced. Maybe someone in the band wanted him gone badly enough to kill him and eliminate the potential problem," Jiff said.

Violet and her car had disappeared. She could have gone missing days later, but the last time Jiff's detective, Ernest could validate anyone seeing her was the night of the murder. The family began to speculate someone had abducted her.

The police maintained Julia was a good suspect for Violet's disappearance as the third person in the lovers' triangle. It didn't help Julia that it played out in the media this way with the help of Violet's parents.

"Violet's parents said in an interview on the air, that Violet came to New Orleans a year ago during a Jazz Fest weekend and met Gervais St. Germain. She fell in love with him and stayed," I said. "Violet could have wanted to kill Gervais because she discovered him sleeping with someone else. The band said she usually followed him around to thwart his attentions with other women. Maybe she felt she was losing control and if she was pregnant, and her hormones were raging, seeing him sleeping with someone else might have pushed her to kill him. It wouldn't be the first crime of passion nor the last."

"You're right. Given the right circumstances and we don't know much about Violet, she could have been pushed over the edge seeing him with someone else," Jiff said. "How would you feel if you saw me with someone else?"

"I don't know. I've really never thought about that until just now," I said. He smiled at me and poured more champagne in our glasses.

I had to wonder, did she drive off that night leaving New Orleans and a lot of memories that weren't working out the way she wanted them to? It would be the irresponsible thing Violet was known to do or was Violet a woman drowning her guilt for killing her lover, or mourning the end of their relationship? Had she met with foul play, or orchestrated her own disappearance? Jiff and I both thought if we found her car, then we might find her. This would help Julia by casting doubt she had anything to do with Violet's disappearance.

Of course, it might not if Violet was found murdered.

The waiter came back to take our order and I wanted another plate of the oysters but was afraid I'd be sending the wrong message to Jiff right about now. I asked the waiter for a recommendation and I went with his suggestion of Steamed Mussels and French Onion Soup.

Jiff ordered Duck Confit, the French Onion Soup also and a Poached Scallop small plate for us to share.

"My mother loves the oysters but the scallops are my favorite and I want you to try them."

"OK, they sound wonderful, but I don't know if they can top the oysters. That is about the best thing I've ever tasted. I just don't think I can eat all this," I said.

"Just taste it. If you like it, you can order it next time," he said. "But, really, save space for the dessert. I asked the chef to make something special just for you."

"We have more questions than answers," I said, turning the conversation back around while we waited for our dinner. "I'm really afraid if we find Violet, she might be the final piece of evidence the police will use in Julia's conviction. I haven't said this to anyone but Julia told me she didn't tell the sequence of events that morning exactly like they happened. Has she told you that?"

"Like what different sequence of events?" Jiff stopped smiling at me and put his glass down on the table, giving me his undivided attention.

I explained what Julia had told me about showering and getting dressed before the police showed up. She didn't remember the dress she wore that night was missing from the room.

"How long have you known this?" he asked.

"She told me this the day she came back after the police questioned her regarding Violet gone missing. She did say when she woke up she wasn't wearing the dress and she didn't take it with her when she left the room. She also said she saw blood when she showered but thought she cut herself. She didn't realize he was dead until she went back up to the room after she dressed and made them some breakfast. I think she was drugged and her accounting of that morning is very foggy."

"I know that and you know that, but now Julia's facts are changing and the police have her in a lie about knowing Violet. This is going to be brutal if we don't find Violet and who killed Gervais."

The waiter brought us a basket of warm French bread, which Jiff handed to me and said, "You have to take a piece. It's baked fresh here."

I picked up and buttered the soft, warm bread. It tasted the way it smelled before ever putting a piece in my mouth. Nothing smells as good as freshly baked bread and when bakeries in New Orleans fire up the ovens the most heavenly aromas are unsuspectingly encountered while driving on the interstate or in certain neighborhoods. This French bread was distracting me from worrying over Julia's lapse in judgment. I took a bite and sat there savoring the melted butter and crusty piece in my mouth.

"I know she should have told you all this and I advised her she needed to update you on everything now. When she told me the morning events weren't exactly like she first said they happened I got a tight feeling in my chest. I'm not ready to believe she did it, but I'm starting to wonder what really happened in that room. I can't even believe I'm saying this." I put another piece of buttered bread on my plate and let it sit there working its magic of warming me with the baked fragrance I could taste without taking a bite.

Jiff paused and looked very pensive before he said, "It's still a little early to make that conclusion," Jiff said, "even though everything keeps coming back to Julia. We need to find Violet and put that piece of the puzzle in place and see where that leads us. This seems like a bunch of disassociated facts or situations that culminated the night Julia decided to live a little," Jiff said.

"I realize her fling with St. Germain moved her from a business relationship to a personal one with him. I can see the police thinking Julia knew Violet, or knew of her," I said.

"Brandy, I've had clients with a lot less evidence against them and they were found guilty. I don't believe she did it but things look bad for Julia."

"Why Jiff, I think you almost like Julia," I smiled.

"You know the hotel business is tough and a lot of work. I admire her for taking it on."

"Yes, she's decided to open her own business so she wouldn't have to answer to anyone ever again after her husband died. Now, she has had to answer to everybody for everything. This isn't fair because she has to work harder and pay to prove she didn't do it," I said.

Our meal came and one thing was better than the next but my favorite was still the oysters. Jiff took a fork full of the scallop dish and fed it to me. It was wonderful, and having a handsome man feed me was intoxicating along with the champagne.

He topped off my glass of champagne and looked serious. "I want to talk to you about something else."

"Sure, what is it?" I reached for my glass.

"I'd like to take our relationship to the next step."

Uh oh, the next step in the relationship discussion. I'm glad I didn't order the oysters.

I think my champagne glass stopped midway from the table to my lips when he said this.

"What I mean is, I'd like for us to spend more time together, maybe go somewhere for a weekend. You know, like a vacation, four or five days. I was thinking Cozumel, Mexico. I love Mexico." Then he stopped talking and waited for my response. I knew I was in trouble.

I started thinking of my sales training. Sales taught that when you were selling something, ask for the sale, and then stop talking. The next person who talked lost. I didn't feel like I was going to lose but I did feel like I was going to relinquish some control depending how I responded. So ask for more info on the deal, see if it's what you really want. This was in sales, of course.

"Really? A weekend trip? When?" I asked.

He smiled. "Yes, I was thinking maybe over the 4th of July weekend."

"That's coming up soon," I said.

"Yes, we both could use a break from all this, don't you think?"

"I would love to take a long weekend with you, I just need a little more planning time. You know the wedding is coming up and I have expenses for that and I'd need to schedule time off." We hadn't spend a night together unless you could count the one Dante thought we spent together—the very short one after a long night of dancing.

"Don't worry about the expenses, just get the time off. I'll get the tickets and the hotel. This is my treat."

"Oh no. I'll pay for my airfare and half of the hotel," I said.

"Look, you never let me pay for anything. You never ask me for anything unless it's to help someone else, like Julia. I can barely buy you dinner when I ask you out. Most…"

"I'm not 'most' and I need some time to plan this if

you want me to spend a weekend with you."

"I'm sorry, I didn't mean anything by that."

I believed him. "I know you didn't mean anything but, I'm not like that," I said. "I pay my own way or I won't go. Labor Day would be better for me if that works for you. By works for you, I mean, I hope you are not in the middle of Julia's trial," I said. "And the wedding would be over and the expenses I have with that."

"OK, deal. I find this independent streak of yours pretty hot," he smiled. "I don't care who pays for what, I just want to spend some time with you in a beautiful place I think we'll both enjoy." He topped off our champagne glasses just as our main course arrived.

A pesky little nudge of my conscious representing Dante guilt had me wondering how this was going to work. Was I really ready to move on? Why was I even asking myself this? Jiff was everything I could ever want, and Dante hadn't made any big attempts, or small ones for that matter, to get me back. He wasn't even speaking to me or calling me.

I fed him a mussel that was bathed in a wonderful wine broth and he fed me a bite of the duck. If the food, the sensual vibe in the restaurant with waiters and a handsome man fawning over me was a drug then I'd be addicted.

"Are you planning on us sleeping together on this trip?" I asked.

I thought he was going to choke since I asked him while he was taking a sip. Instead, he placed his champagne glass on the table and wiped his mouth with his napkin. He cleared his throat and looked at me in the eye, "Well, I hope you would consider us finding out more about each other, and if I'm lucky enough for our relationship to take that step, then I'd be a happy man."

"I bet you're great in court. You are good when you are put on the spot. Fast thinker, diplomatic, cool under fire." I smiled.

"Thanks. Was that a test?"

"Not a test, just an honest question."

"Oh yeah, well I would also like for you to come meet my family next weekend. We're having a family birthday dinner for my sister at my parents' house."

Wait. What? I felt our little love aura exploding.

"Your parents' house? On Audubon Place? Meet your family? Before we go on our trip? What if they don't like me, or what if we don't get along over that weekend trip? Isn't this out of order? Shouldn't we do that weekend trip first?" I was flummoxed. His dad's house was a mansion on a private street with a guard shack that was bigger than my apartment. His family was old money and had lots of it.

I could call and meet CEOs and boardrooms full of people, but meeting someone's family—his parents—was alien to me. I'd grown up next door to Dante and his family. I never had to meet anyone's family I dated. I just had to put up with them sticking their noses in all of my business. Jiff had five brothers and a sister. Sisters hate girlfriends. Jiff's parents were a power couple. His Mom was a judge, and his Dad was a very wealthy trial attorney, a take-no-prisoners, scorched-earth sort of practitioner. He was often on the news. Dante's mother was a housewife who used to scream at her five boys until she passed out. His dad was in construction and was always trying to figure out how to add another room onto their home. Jiff's family had staff to help run their offices and lives.

And then what? He would want to meet my family. This had to be post-poned…indefinitely. The Alexander clan got A+ in dysfunction and God help me if my crazy uncle or any of my relatives were visiting when this happened. What if it was a holiday and my dad pulled out that carving knife? I was way out in front of my headlights on this one.

The waiter brought over two cups with saucers and a pot of freshly brewed coffee and chicory. He poured the coffee into my cup and it smelled just like the coffee Miss Ruth—Dante's mother—dripped every morning. The first whiff of the brew reminded me of all those early mornings Dante and I used to sit on my porch drinking his mother's coffee together. That whiff also sent a pang of guilt with it that I was somehow betraying all of them, especially Dante's mother.

"OK, take a deep breath and let's just finish our wonderful meal," Jiff said bringing me back to the present. "Forget about my family and dinner for now. I can see this was a little too much to spring on you all at once. You look a little overwhelmed with the vacation and now my folks. They are very nice people, by the way, and they are anxious to meet you. But, let's just have dessert. I asked them to make your favorite thing in the whole world…king cake," he said giving me his adoring smile— the smile that made me go find him at the end of a parade—the smile that melted me to my core while pushing thoughts of Dante, and Jiff's family, out of my head.

Chapter Fourteen

TWO DAYS AFTER our dinner at Feelings, Jiff called a status meeting in his office with Julia for 9:00 a.m. to go over everything he knew and didn't know.

I agreed to pick her up and go with her to the meeting. When I arrived she was dressed and waiting in the foyer checking herself out front and back in the gold leaf, Louis XIV floor to ceiling mirror at the front door.

"Good morning," I said trying to sound upbeat and not like a cheerleader. "You look nice today. That's a beautiful suit, is it new?" I asked.

"Yes, it's new. Frank made it for me," she said while she picked imaginary lint off her jacket and then leaned in to check her teeth making sure she didn't have anything stuck in them.

She was partially her old self. The suit was tailored to fit her perfectly and well made. I thought I might have to hire Frank as my wardrobe consultant.

"Where's your purse?" I asked.

"Frank's bringing it. He'll be down in a minute. We can wait in the car."

"What do you mean, Frank's bringing it? Is he coming with us?" I asked.

"Yes, I need him for moral support." Julia said.

"I thought you had me for moral support," I said.

Woozie appeared and gave us each a cup of coffee in a go cup. "Take this. Where Frank at? He gonna make you late. I bet he putting on lip gloss. That only gonna get him in trouble, that lady makeup." She turned to the stairwell and yelled, "FRANK!"

"Lip gloss?" I asked.

"I told you, he's a metrosexual," Julia said still looking in the mirror now fluffing her hair.

"I think you confusing the 'o' in metrosexual with the 'o' in homosexual." Woozie said looking at Julia and putting a big emphasis on the 'o' in both words.

"Julia, a metrosexual is someone you would date and you both would be happy comparing your wardrobes but not your makeup." She looked at me as if I had two heads. "If Frank is coming he has to get down here, now. We'll wait in the car." I thanked Woozie for the coffee, kissed her hello and goodbye, and headed outside to my BMW. I unlocked my doors with the electronic key and both clicked open. Julia got in on the passenger side without a rebuttal.

Frank appeared running down the front steps with his jacket and Julia's purse fluttering around him.

"He's like having your own personal Sherpa," I said to Julia before he got in the car. She acted like she didn't hear me.

"OK, I have your purse, hand cream, tissues, makeup, hairspray…I think I have everything," Frank said out of breath as he tried to squeeze into the back seat behind Julia. He was carrying Julia's purse along with a satchel of his own that he wore with the strap across his chest— New York style.

"We're meeting her attorney, not auditioning for a lead role with Hollywood South," I said, checking him out in the rear view mirror. He had on a lot of eyeliner and eyebrow pencil, but no lipstick, thank God.

Julia had become so distraught and preoccupied over the last few weeks that I'd asked Frank to move into the bed and breakfast and stay with her 24/7. I instructed him to help her keep appointments and make sure she looked presentable when she had to go somewhere. Between Frank and Woozie, they kept an eye on Julia when I couldn't be there and they reported to me if she looked like she was starting a meltdown. Woozie kept both Frank and Julia on a tight schedule and Julia from feeling sorry for herself. Frank was her wardrobe consultant and hairdresser. He kept her from showing up in a bathrobe— her outfit of choice lately. She was convinced she was going to be found guilty of murder and could think of nothing else, therefore, decision-making went out the window.

Woozie had called about a week ago to tell me Julia had started drinking her breakfast so she hid all the liquor. I told Woozie to make her breakfast and make the orange juice look like a Mimosa by watering down the juice with Perrier water. I said put a little umbrella in it to make it look like one. If Julia wanted coffee with a hit of whisky, I suggested Woozie rub the Jameson's around the rim of the cup but don't put any in it. If this didn't work, I thought I might have to get Julia medicated. I thought I remembered seeing a few Valium in my mother's medicine cabinet. Woozie reported that it seemed to be working because Julia wasn't complaining.

Ernest and Michelle were waiting at Jiff's office when I arrived with Julia and Frank. The receptionist stood and said she would show us to the conference room. I asked Frank to wait in the reception area. He didn't say a word but stiffened his posture, did a little fast shake of his head as if being excluded didn't bother him. He sat down and we left him busying himself looking for something in his satchel.

The conference room had floor to ceiling windows with the same spectacular view of the bends in the river that Jiff's office had. There was coffee, juice and croissants on the credenza at one end of the room and the receptionist said we should help ourselves. Ernest and I went straight for the coffee. When Jiff came in with his stenographer, they each took a seat at one end of the table. She sat away from the conference table behind Jiff but in our view so we could all see her and be reminded that this was being documented. We all took a seat, Julia closest to Jiff with me next to her on one side of the table and Ernest sat next to Michelle on the other side, opposite us. Jiff thanked us all for coming, advised us he was documenting the meeting and began.

"Julia we want to update you on where we are and if there is anything new you have recalled since our last meeting. Please feel free to speak openly in here. I think you know Ernest and this is Michelle, his assistant, also on my team," Jiff nodded at Ernest and Michelle. Julia and Michelle nodded hello at the introductions.

"Yes, I know everyone now," Julia answered.

"If there is anything of a confidential nature I will ask the others to leave the room because they don't have attorney-client privilege. Understand."

"Yes. Can I ask a question?" Julia said.

"Of course, go right ahead," Jiff answered.

"What can be done about the media?" she asked. She went on to say every few days another newsworthy update on Violet's disappearance would interrupt normal broadcasting with breaking news of a body found in some desolate spot off the Chef Menteur Highway. Then the film crew would zoom in on crime-scene officials pulling the body out of the marsh. The news would then break into normal programming at a later time and advise, "The body recovered on the Chef Menteur was identified and it is not Violet Fornet. Violet Fornet is still missing."

"Yes, something can be done. Stop watching the news." Jiff answered her. "You are their subject of interest du jour and watching the news is going to be depressing until this turns around or until the press find something or someone more interesting to report on."

"Of course, they never updated the viewing public as to the identity of the person. They just reported a body even if they knew early on it wasn't even a woman," Julia said.

We all had been seeing the photos of Violet as a happy child playing with friends or in school on the media updates. Interruptions into the normal programming would be repeated during the scheduled news broadcast advising viewers that an exhaustive search of the parks in the city turned up nothing.

A few days later the news, with another smiling, happy photo of Violet, would advise that the Coast Guard helicopters had done a grid search over Lake Pontchartrain that produced nothing. Then the NOPD brought out the search and rescue dogs to canvass along the I-10 in New Orleans East trying to ascertain if she'd been dumped there. Of course, as soon as the media showed the latest citywide attempt to find Violet, they would cut to the grieving family, crying and holding another vigil.

This went on until the end of the month when the national news had picked it up. For every flattering photo of Violet as a cute, happy, person with a full life ahead of her flashed on screen, there was a driver's license type photo of Julia as the person of interest in her disappearance as well as the accused in the upcoming St. Germain murder trial. Sometimes the news would focus on the St. Germain murder, and show a photo of Violet and her loving finance' whose future had been dashed by a character like Julia. The media would take a photo of the bed and breakfast and portray Julia as a wealthy interloper who dashed the happiness of Violet Fornet and Gervais St. Germain. The press portrayed Julia in a series of unflattering photos—how did they even find these—in articles murdering Gervais in a jealous rage, and as a person of interest in the abduction/disappearance of Violet Fornet.

"The fact that Violet is missing and there was no proof of abduction does not thwart the media speculation. It's just speculation at this point, so stop watching the news," Jiff stated. We all nodded in agreement. Jiff went on to say, "The bigger issue which does not bode well for you, Julia is that the police have proof that you did know Violet. This is the fodder the press, not to mention the prosecution, is eating up."

"What can we do about it?" I asked.

"Find Violet and prove Julia had nothing to do with her disappearance," Ernest said.

"There's still the matter of Gervais St. Germain, and the media is using Violet to push that agenda. The family keeps poking the news reporters with a stick to keep it stirred up and they are seen as sympathetic. We all feel sorry for them. Her family doesn't know Violet was a skank," Michelle added.

"We have no control over what they report. We can only give friendly reporter information to help us. Ernest? You have something?" Jiff asked.

Ernest began, "Someone in the NOPD finally thought to check the crime cameras."

He went to the DVD player in the room, popped in a disc and hit play. "It'll come up here in a second."

"Yes, these are the crime cameras originally deployed to catch criminals but since catching criminals cost money, the cameras had been repurposed in order to pay for themselves. Now, the crime cameras were being used to fund the city coffers under the guise of digitally ticketing drivers with speeding violations. I suspect this was the underlying motive to get the public to embrace them in the first place," Jiff said.

"Well, lo and behold, there's Violet's clunker of a car, an old Dodge, with a shark's open mouth painted on the trunk and BITE ME under it for all to see, cruising down Harrison Avenue toward the park at exactly 4:45 a.m. on the day Gervais was murdered," Ernest said. The time stamped video showed a night view on Harrison Avenue of her car. You could see only one person in the car driving—Violet. She wasn't driving fast or in a straight line, but she was driving.

Michelle said, "She didn't sleep it off for very long if that's what she told her friend when they left that bar."

"The media and the family have already seen this footage. I know why it didn't air. My friend in the department who gave me this copy said they could not conclusively ascertain whether or not there was another person in the vehicle. The family is keeping pressure on the department to follow up on the abduction angle," Ernest said.

Jiff said, "This is the break we were looking for."

"How?" Julia and I asked simultaneously.

"Well, there is no one following her. Watch the tape. The time lapses for five minutes before you see another car, and it's a police car, not Julia's vehicle," Jiff answered.

Michelle said, "No wonder the police weren't in a hurry to cough this up. Violet's family is keeping the pressure on the NOPD and the media to find Violet. They were in the area and they look bad if foul play was afoot and they missed it."

"I'll do a search from this last known point in the direction she's driving," Ernest said, "and see if we can't locate that car. She had a lot to drink, and if the time is correct, 4:45 a.m., then she got into the car and started driving. I'll check with the banks along Harrison, maybe they have cameras that could add to this footage and we'll see if she stopped or turned. They might have a better photo shot that will tell if anyone else was in the car, even though I doubt there was."

"Well, that direction means she drove into City Park through the golf course," said Jiff.

"Yes, but there are several places where she could have gone off the road and no one would have spotted her car," Michelle added.

Jiff said, "Get right on this, Ernest, I want to find her before the police do."

Ernest was busy pulling out a map of New Orleans and putting a red dot on the site where Violet was last seen on the camera. "This is the path she was moving.

There's a couple of canals and Bayou St. John along Harrison. If she turned off Harrison, that's all residential and someone would have noticed her or picked her up on their security cameras. I'll reach out to the area's crime prevention network. I'll ask them to send out an email blast to see if anyone has footage of car burglaries or home invasions, etc. They can let us know if she did turn off before she hit the park. If she drove and turned on to Marconi, that will be harder. She could have gone in anywhere along there. Maybe we get a diver or two in the water and take a look. I'm sure there might be a few cars at the bottom from Katrina so let's see if her car is in there too."

"Good plan. Make it happen," Jiff said.

"I'm on it," Ernest answered.

Chapter Fifteen

I HADN'T VISITED my parents since the big wedding announcement. If I remembered correctly, my mother would be at Pilates and my dad would be home alone. I found him tinkering on one of the cars in the garage behind the house.

"Hey there, don't I know you?" Dad asked as he leaned and kissed me on the cheek.

"I see you're in your office working on matters of national security," I teased back. "I have a surprise for you." I produced the bottle of Chianti I was holding behind my back and presented it to him. "Isn't this the same wine you had the night the Fortunatas were here?"

He took the bottle. "Yeah, this is it. I've been nursing along the last glass of what was left in the bottle Donnato left me. He says he's the only one in the city that has this wine. He has a cousin in Italy that makes this Chianti at his vineyard and they don't ship to anyone else outside of Italy." He turned the bottle and pointing to the back of it said, "See the label on the back of the bottle, right here it says it's from the Fortunata family's vineyard. Where did you get it?"

"One of my clients is the wholesaler who imports it for Mr. Donnato." I read the label and looked at it closely. "That's impressive their family name is right here on it. Apparently, his cousin is shipping him a boatload of it for Angela's wedding. My client doesn't drink Chianti so he gave it to me. Where is everybody?"

"Thanks, I'm glad to know I'll get some of this at the wedding." He was selecting a ratchet wrench for the vehicular problem he was working on. "Your mother is rolling around on some giant beach ball in some exercise class and your sister went to the movies with Dante's two younger brothers, you know, the twins. I think one of them has a thing for Sherry."

"Which one? Maybe Miss Ruth could get a marriage to one of her boys out of our family yet," I said.

"I can't keep their names straight except Dante's. It's one of them whose name starts with a D".

"Dad, all their names start with a D. Dante, Danny, Dennis, Darren and Darryl. The twins are Darren and Darryl," I said.

"Well then, it's one of them twins. Miss Ruth comes over here crying to your mother all the time over you and Dante. She's cries you broke Dante's heart. She cries Dante screwed it up by waiting too long to ask you to marry him. She cries because you don't live here anymore. She cries every time your name is mentioned. You can't imagine what I have to listen to. Now she has your mother worried you and Dante aren't getting married." His voice became muffled when he lay down on his Craftsman Metal Creeper and rolled under the car to work.

"Miss Ruth is crying over something all the time. She doesn't need Dante and me as an excuse. What do you think, Dad? What do you think about Dante and me getting married? Do you think we belong together?" I raised my voice and talked down into the car engine so he could hear me.

He rolled out from under the car and looked at me. "If you love him, marry him. If you don't, move on." He rolled back under the car.

"One minute he says he doesn't want to lose me then I don't hear from him for weeks on end. I never know what he's thinking," I said.

"That's funny. Last week Dante came over here and helped me change the oil on your sister's car. He said the same thing about you."

"Really? He comes over here to talk to you?" I asked.

"I think he wanted to see if I thought he still had a chance with you. I told him the two of you needed to get away from all of us—both families—and see how you feel about each other. You know, as my old friend Frank Davis used to say, are you gonna fish or cut bait?" He started to roll back under the car but stopped and asked, "What have you done with Woozie? I have to eat your mother's cooking. Get her back over here or you and I are going to have a problem."

"Woozie is needed for the greater good at Julia's right now. She'll be back. Didn't you know Mom couldn't cook when you married her?"

"Of course I did. I didn't marry her because she could cook." Then he rolled back under the car. A horrifying visual of my parents having sex flashed through my mind and I shook my head to clear it. After a few seconds of awkward silence the conversation picked back up.

"Anyway," I started, "there is so much going against Julia and while there are a bunch of people with a motive to kill that guy, the police are convinced Julia is guilty."

"What do you think?" he asked.

"The police found her in a lie, and you know, that's

not good. Every time some new fact is revealed it isn't in her favor. My gut says she's innocent but everything, and I mean everything else, says she did it."

"Go with your gut, that's always worked for me," he said.

I stayed in the garage handing him tools he asked for so he didn't have to roll out, get up, look for something, then roll back under. We stayed on more universal topics after that, such as did he think the Pilates class was making my mom look better, or was Sherry interested in one of the twins or did she just go out with them for something to do? I asked him if she ever went anywhere with just one of them. Dad said no, always the pair. Finally, he announced he "got it", whatever it was he was trying to get, he rolled out and got up, putting away the tools he had accumulated under the car. When he finished he said, "C'mon, let's go inside. I want to have a glass of that Chianti with my daughter."

"You still plan on going to Angela's wedding, right?" I asked.

"You know we wouldn't miss that mega-dago party for all the gold Italian horns in Little Italy. Your mother has been buying and trying on dresses to show me so I can tell her which one looks the best on her. Problem is, I don't remember what the last one looked like before she's standing in front of me wearing another one and asking me which one I like better. She must have ten dresses in there and she plans to return all but one. Can't you come over here and help her with that?"

"Do you really think that's a good idea? She and I will only end up in a fight and we will drag you into it. Sherry is much better at fashion than I am. Remember, Dad, she went to school for fashion design. She should help Mom." Sherry, my sister, did go to school for fashion design, but changed her major at least five times since then. I didn't want to get roped into telling my mother what looked good on her and what didn't. Dad didn't want to do it either.

"Yeah, you're probably right. Sherry is a better choice. Well, are you ever going to bring that new guy you are dating around here and let us meet him?" he asked.

"You think that's a good idea with Dante next door?"

"Oh, yeah. That might be bad if Miss Ruth pops in while you're here with him. Then she'll be crying over that."

I didn't want to tell him Dante had already seen Jiff at my apartment early one morning and I didn't want him blowing a gasket seeing me parade in and out of my parents' house with him. "I'm bringing Jiff, that's the new guy's name, as my date to the wedding so you can meet him there." I thought this would be a great time to expose him to my family. It would be in short bursts without too much time spent with my dad grilling him on what he did, why he did it and who he did it with. My mother would be busy keeping an eye on my sister, Sherry and the Deedler twins, trying to figure out which one was trying to corrupt her. Hopefully, the music would be so loud they really couldn't do much more than nod hello and shake hands. This would get the pesky matter of meeting my family out of the way.

It was late when I drove home and I had the feeling I was being followed again. I kept an eye on my rear view mirror. A car pulled out behind me when I left my Dad's. It stayed a few lengths back and when I turned onto my block, it stopped at the corner and cut the lights while I parked. This stuff with Julia and Violet was starting to make me paranoid. I hurried inside as my three dogs were raising a ruckus barking. No one was going to sneak up on me in my own home, not while they were around.

Chapter Sixteen

J IFF CALLED MY office at 11:15 a.m. the next day. I thought he was going to ask me to lunch, but instead he said to meet him at the corner of Harrison Avenue and Wisner Boulevard as soon as possible. The divers had found something.

He told me not to draw any attention to the location or tell anyone where I was going. I left my downtown parking garage and inched along downtown streets in the Central Business District, under the sweltering sun, trying to avoid inhaling bus exhaust from the lumbering behemoth ahead of me I couldn't seem to pass. I made it to the section of Canal Street, just a few blocks from downtown where the street becomes lined with magnificent ancient oak trees giving a canopy of shade affording a more pleasant drive. Canal runs from the Mississippi River to Lake Pontchartrain across the entire city. I can remember only once Canal was blocked due to a fire and the fire trucks. You just had to turn off Canal, go one or two blocks over and run parallel to your final destination. Simple, fast, easy. The interstate is faster unless there's been an eighteen-wheeler overturned, an accident or a visiting dignitary and the entire stretch from the airport to downtown is shut down—both ways—to on and off traffic. I prefer the scenic route over the concrete route any day and Canal Street's overly wide stretch with the streetcars clanging and rumbling up the neutral ground has a soothing effect that the cars going 80+ mph on I-10 just can't replicate. Once I turned off of Canal by City Park Avenue I was in the heart of the cemeteries on either side of me until I hit Esplanade Avenue. This was the bayou end of Esplanade, the opposite end from our pedicab ride to Feelings of the other night and it was no less beautiful. Homes on this end were large and graceful, but not mansions. I was starting to get lost in thoughts over our dinner that night, and about meeting his parents, and going on a weekend trip with him when Bayou St. John appeared and I was brought back to the business at hand. A dark thought crossed my mind sending a shiver down my spine in this heat, and I decided to check my rear view mirror to watch for anyone following me. The majestic oaks shading my previous route opened up to the sun now in my eyes as I followed the bayou toward the lake. The bayou's serene flat surface was home to ducks and a canoe rental business. I drove along with City Park on my left, and the New Orleans Museum of Art sitting back like the grand dame of New Orleans she is, at the end of a long driving mall. The park grounds opened up this area even more with all its oaks, magnolias and pine trees. These were landscaped around walking paths and bike trails that framed my drive all the way over the Wisner overpass where I got a great view of the golf course on the left, the lake straight ahead and the Gentilly neighborhood on my right. This street had a lot less traffic and I was sure there was no one following me here. Just to be sure, I passed my turn, went a few blocks, and made a U-turn back to the street Jiff told me to take. If a car was following me, it would have to make the U-turn and I would spot it. It looked clear so I turned over the bridge into Gentilly to where Jiff directed me to park. He told me not to park on Wisner or Harrison but go over the Bayou St. John Bridge; turn left and go to the end of Davey Street where I should see a black van there with a dive flag on the side. That's where I would meet them.

When I got to the meeting spot, Jiff and Ernest were standing with two divers looking at footage taken on a video camera. The divers were standing there dripping wet, still in their neoprene dive skins and operating a video camera in a waterproof housing with the most enormous lighting gear on it I had ever seen.

"Welcome to Hollywood Deep South," Ernest joked.

"Yes, we foolishly go where those with more sense think better of," replied one of the divers who introduced himself as Hardware. Hardware operated the camera equipment. The other diver was peeling off his dive skin to his waist, toweling off and put on a T-shirt that said, *Divers Do It Deeper* on the back. Ernest introduced him as Jake.

"What, no nickname?" I asked.

"No, just Jake, but you can call me whatever you want," Jake said smiling.

"Easy there fella, she's his squeeze," Ernest said nodding toward Jiff.

Hardware queued the video back to the beginning. We all watched the small screen. There were no images, only darkness until the strobes illuminated an object the camera aimed directly at. The only sound on the recording was the divers breathing through their regulators. It was creepy and sinister watching the video of what was mostly dark water with darker objects in it until the lights bounced off something big, like a rusted motorcycle frame missing a wheel or a large car or truck engine. One skiff with a giant hole in it was upside down on the bottom along with several car bumpers and fenders partially submerged in the silt. All kinds of junk scrolled past the viewfinder along with numerous bicycles or metal chairs in distorted and twisted shapes. When the divers' fins touched the bottom, silt clouds mushroomed and billowed around them cutting the vision to zero. They would slowly swim away from that spot and find undisturbed, dark water to film. Then something very large loomed out of the darkness. A white rusted object came into view and I recognized it as a van resting on its side. The diver-cameraman swam in a circle around it to capture the license plate while his dive buddy went to work, tying a line with a float he sent to the surface above it, marking the location. Then they continued to swim on slowly looking for another treasure. They repeated this and marked about five more cars until the open shark mouth popped into the viewfinder and there was a sudden jerk of the camera. Everyone started laughing and the diver who was shooting the video said, "Man, that surprised the hell outta me. Why didn't you tell me what it looked like?"

"That would have ruined the fun," Ernest said.

"Looks like you found it. Where exactly is it?" I asked.

"Keep watching," Jiff said.

The divers circled the vehicle and there inside, still in her seat belt, was Violet. I caught my breath and my hand went to my chest.

"Oh, I'm sorry, I should have warned you. These guys told us she was still in the car," Jiff said.

The video took several minutes to document all parts of the vehicle exactly the way it looked and how it was positioned. It looked like it drove straight into the bayou and came to a stop on the bottom. It was upright on all four tires resting in about fifteen feet of water. The divers didn't mark or touch it, but instead came up and videoed the landmarks showing its position to the bridge, road and water's edge.

"We only tag vehicles that didn't have anyone in them," the diver named Jake said. "Some may have floated in there from Katrina and others are probably insurance claims dumped here hoping no one ever finds them. The police can figure out what's what from the VIN numbers if they can locate any that haven't rusted off or been removed," said one of the divers.

"That's clearly Violet or someone in her car with no one else," Ernest said.

"And she was driving," Jiff said. "That suggests there was no foul play."

"My money is she was drunk and she fell asleep at the wheel," Ernest said. "I'll get my uncle's dredging company out here. I want us to control the pulling out of these vehicles. I've already told him that we might need his help here and he's all for it. You know he's good on camera. He said he'd like to give that family closure by finding their daughter. I'll make a call to the news stations as soon as he gets here and sets up." Ernest walked away from us dialing his cell phone.

"The police are going to want to send down their own divers, don't you think?" I asked.

"We work for the police department," Hardware said. "I owe Ernest a favor. We'll say we were here spearfishing and found that vehicle. I'll call it in when you give me the go ahead." Smiling, his dive buddy held up two spear guns.

"Hardware, call it in to Detective Deedler. It's his case and it might buy us some good will if he knows we let him take the credit," Jiff added.

Ɵ Ɵ Ɵ

I ASKED JIFF why he was being so nice to Dante. He explained he thought Dante did Julia a favor calling us in and showing his hand with the questions surrounding the missing person's report on Violet. Dante gave us a heads up and returning the favor, so to speak, made us look like nice guys. Jiff said Dante was going to find out anyway and there was nothing for us to gain by taking the credit. I wasn't much for sharing goodwill with Dante at the moment. He hadn't bothered to call or say hello. For all I knew he was handcuffed to Hanky Panky right now.

The dredging company arrived with two trucks and set up, ready to launch into pulling those vehicles out of the bayou when the TV news channels started to arrive. They were lowering heavy cables into the water when the police, and by police I mean my two favorites—Dante and Hanky—arrived. I was on the other side of the bayou behind the dive van but I could see the vein pumping in Dante's neck from where I stood when he spotted me with Jiff.

Ernest's uncle, Noble Jacques St. Amant of Thibodeaux, Louisiana, owned the largest dredging company in the South. He had pulled cars, trains, sunken boats, ships, barges; you name it, out of just about every body of water south of the Mason Dixon line. His company and bravado were second to none. Once asked if his real first name was Noble, he answered, "Cher, my family are descendants of Louis King of France. We were all noblemen so we're all given the first name of Noble. You have to use our middle name with it so forty Cajuns don't turn around when you yell, hey Noble." When Noble Jacques St. Amant arrived, he ran the show. He was perfect for the camera and the news people loved him.

Ernest drew the attention of a popular reporter and brought her over to meet Uncle Noble. In his charming Cajun accent—he laid it on a little thicker when on camera—he told the reporter just where to set her cameras for the best footage when he started pulling the vehicles out of the water. Other TV stations and crews were racing around trying to determine what their best vantage spot was.

"Now, Chere, you listen to me. You are gonna want to get better shots at the first few that I pull outta dat dere bayou, but don't you move, Chere. Don't give up your front row spot for the cheap seats. You stay put, ma petite, and you will get the best shot of Violet Fornet's vehicle. C'est bon," he said putting his arm around the reporter and walking her to the perfect viewing spot. The other reporters and cameramen scampered around to stake out their positions.

One reporter interviewed Noble and asked him why he was offering his services without charge to the City of New Orleans. "If it was my daughter," he answered, "I'd want to find her. If I can help give these people some peace or closure, then God would want me to render my assistance. These folks need peace." With that he marched off to instruct his workmen about securing the dredges. He told them to use the hydraulic winches rather than the grab bucket. He had told us earlier the grab bucket can smash a car and he didn't want the family traumatized if Violet's car came up mangled. The scuba divers geared up to go in. Their job at this point was going to be to hook the vehicles so the dredge could winch them out of the bayou.

Noble Jacques didn't disappoint the press. After pulling out a Jeep, the van on its side and a Lincoln Continental, the divers hooked the Shark-mobile and it slowly emerged from its watery grave. Her family was there and when they saw the body in the car, Violet's mother fainted. Dante and his partner were there and commandeered the vehicle as soon as it was free of the winch and the forensics people went right to work. What couldn't be discounted was that she was driving, still in her seat belt and there was no one else in the car.

Jiff, Ernest and I kept a low profile, out of sight as much as possible. Jiff had his own cameraman taking videos of Violet's vehicle recovery for their use in court, if it came to that.

"I feel really bad for Violet's family having to see her like that. What a way to find a lost child," I said to Jiff and Ernest.

"They lost Violet long before she ever drove into that bayou," said Ernest.

After a couple of hours of documenting everything that happened and interviewing all the key people involved, the news media packed up and left. Jiff and Ernest went and thanked Noble and his company for their assistance in finding Violet. It had taken them a couple of hours to locate her and remove her from the watery grave. The police department took the credit for finding Violet since it was their divers who found her while spearfishing.

The police recovered Violet's belongings in the trunk. Dante told the press it looked like her clothes in a suitcase and a couple of tote bags were in the trunk. Ernest's police buddies told him what Dante did not tell the press. Also found hidden in the wheel well was an airtight bag of cocaine.

The coroner's report showed the cause of death was drowning.

I thought if Gervais St. Germain had invited Violet to stay with him at the bed and breakfast, they'd both be alive, stoned of course, but alive, and Julia wouldn't be in the middle of this fiasco. The press wasn't ready to let Julia completely off the hook even though there wasn't any evidence of foul play involved in Violet's disappearance. They still made her out to be the home wrecker and further speculated Julia's relationship with St. Germain is perhaps what drove Violet to commit suicide by running off the road into the bayou. The cocaine and the night of drinking were not mentioned in their news report. Julia really needed a break in the news. Where were our politicians who make national newsworthy sexual and corrupt blunders when we needed them?

But who killed Gervais St. Germain? Violet was driving herself into Bayou St. John at the time of his death so she couldn't have killed him. Witnesses put her in the bar until 4:30 a.m. Julia still looked good for the St. Germain murder.

Now more than ever.

Chapter Seventeen

I STOPPED BY Julia's bed and breakfast to pick up my dress and stuff it into my car for the photo shoot. The Fortunata Tuddo-rama was scheduled to take up the next two days of my life starting with the wedding party photos at 4:00 p.m. followed by the rehearsal dinner.

Woozie answered the door before I could knock. She greeted me with, "Miz Julia is more down than ever. You gotta help Frank and me lift her spirits."

"You haven't let her have any of the Jameson's, have you?" I asked.

"No. I still rubbing it around the rim of her coffee mug like you said to."

"Where is she?" Woozie led me upstairs to Julia's apartment that took up the rear of the building over the kitchen. She was sitting at her desk, staring out of the window. Frank was sitting in the chair across from her idly flipping through a Cosmopolitan magazine.

"Hey, Julia, what are you wearing to the wedding? I know you don't want to miss seeing *Gone With The Wind* meets the *Godfather*. I think it's all being filmed as a reality TV show."

"It's more like Scarlett O'Hara meets the American Mafia," Frank said looking up from his magazine. I saw one corner of Julia's mouth turn up as she resisted a smile.

Before she could answer and say she wasn't going, Frank jumped out of the chair and said, "I've been working non-stop making her this to wear." In a grand gesture he threw open the doors of her armoire, parted the hanging garments, and pulled out a black silk, calf-length dress with a sheer bodice. He held it high in the air with one hand while sweeping his other arm behind it to present it for all of us to admire. It was beautifully made and would look stunning on Julia. "In fact, I almost have the dress for Woozie ready if she would only stop working long enough for a last minute fitting." He hung Julia's dress on the top of the door and I went over to scrutinize it more closely.

"I'm wearing that bridesmaid's disaster of a dress that makes me look like a Mardi Gras float and you get to wear this?" I was in awe of Frank's talent. I looked from Julia to Woozie and back. "Both of you are lucky Frank is doing this for you. You know, Frank, if they don't appreciate you, please come live with me." After inspecting the precision stitches on Julia's gown, I asked Frank, "What kind of machine do you use to sew this silk?"

"I don't have a machine. I sew everything by hand," he answered.

"By hand?" I couldn't believe how perfect every stitch was.

"He cuts his own patterns after taking our measurements," Julia added. Maybe she realized she hadn't been appreciating Frank's skills as much as she should have or maybe she thought Frank might take me up on my offer to poach him.

Frank was back in the armoire flipping through the hangers one by one until he found what he was looking for. I felt like I was in a high-end fashion boutique with Frank, the salesperson, showing us what to wear. With another dramatic whirlwind of fabric fluttering out of the closet, he swept another dress over his arm displaying what he made for Woozie. It was a soft, flowing peach chiffon that still needed to be hemmed.

"Woozie, what are you waiting for?" I asked. "Put it on now so Frank can hem it. The wedding is tomorrow."

"Why I get a peach color and Julia get black? Ain't I sexy enough for black?" Woozie demanded of Frank with her hands on her hips. "You shoulda made my dress black and Julia peach. Now, everyone is gonna call her the Black Widow woman at that wedding."

"Do you see what I have to deal with?" Frank asked me. "They tag team me all day long," Frank sniffed as if he was completely worn down.

"No one is going to call her that. Come on, Woozie, go put the dress on so I can see how pretty you make it look and Frank can hem it," I said. "Y'all are all acting like we're going to a funeral instead of a wedding." No one moved. "Well, I'm adjusting the attitude in here, right now."

"Good luck with that, girlfriend, cuz I'm tired of trying," Frank said over his shoulder as he followed Woozie behind a dressing screen at one end of the room to zip her up.

I found just the ticket in Julia's album of CDs and popped in *She Drives Me Crazy* by the Fine Young Cannibals and started dancing around the room. I pulled Julia to her feet and tried to make her laugh saying something silly, "You know I only dance on two occasions and that is when I'm alone or with someone." She was slow to acquiesce but who can refuse FYC? Frank came out from behind the screen jutting his head from side to side in time with each deliberate step he took to the music. He led Woozie by one hand with the other hand on his waist and bent up at the wrist as he moved it opposite every step. He sort of looked like a rooster prancing around the barnyard. He had Woozie step up on a footstool so he could pin the hem. While Julia and I danced, Woozie started moving her hips and shoulders to the music. Frank stood and gave up hemming the dress and joined us dancing around the room. Woozie stayed on the pedestal continuing to groove along.

We all laughed while we danced with arms in the air, moving and hip bumping each other. Before the song ended and while Frank twirled Julia around, I booted up a couple more CD's, all dance songs that kept us moving around aerobically for the next thirty minutes. Finally, Woozie bailed and had to sit down but did keep doing dance moves from her seat. She watched, laughing while Frank changed dance partners every few steps with Julia and I—swinging, spinning or dipping us. Julia was into the music by now and we laughed and danced like fools for almost an hour.

"That was fun," Julia said collapsing on her bed. "Who's playing at the wedding?"

Uh oh, I thought she was going to sink into a black depression when I told her what band was going to be there, so instead I said, "There are eighteen groomsmen, Italian groomsmen, who will be looking to dance. You don't want to miss that, do you?"

"I don't want to miss it," Frank said putting pins in his mouth getting ready to resume hemming Woozie's dress.

"I don't know." Julia balked. "People all know this

big murder mess is still going on and they think I'm a murderess."

"You gonna go cuz I got this great dress and you got that great dress and when they sees us they gonna know you no killer," Woozie said stepping back up on the stool after admiring herself in the full length mirror. "I look good in this here dress. We both going to this here wedding."

"Well, I do need to get out of here and Frank can come, right?" Julia asked.

"Of course, you, Frank and Woozie can all come to the wedding together. Besides, Julia, do you want to miss the potential fireworks with Jiff, Dante, Hanky and me all in the same room at the same time?"

"Well, I won't know where to look first, at the Italians or you and your cluster of chaos," Julia said pulling out a pair of shoes from a bottom drawer in the armoire to wear with her dress.

Frank was busy hemming Woozie's dress with a mouthful of pins and would mumble something that sounded like 'turn', which Woozie did every so often as the pins went in adjusting the length of her gown. I almost hated to ask, "Frank, what are you wearing?"

He put all the pins back in the pincushion one at a time before he answered. By now, all three of us had eyes on Frank waiting for the answer. "I made myself a seersucker suit which I can wear all summer after the wedding," he said.

"Oh, good. That sounds nice. Yes, that will look great." Woozie, Julia and I all answered talking over each other at the same time.

"Oh, look at the time, I've got to get to Angela's for

the photos. Frank, where's my bridesmaid's dress?"

Frank went to find my dress and while he was gone, I said to Julia, "Make sure he shows up dressed like a man, and not wearing makeup or carrying a purse."

"You sound like you think Frank is gay," Julia said.

"He gay," Woozie answered.

Frank returned with my bridesmaid's dress and offered to help me get it in the car.

"Don't be surprised if your dress fits a little better," he said looking sheepish as we walked downstairs and out to my car. "I altered it to make you look gorgeous, even though I couldn't do anything about that putrid color."

"The only way this dress could make me look gorgeous is if you burned the original dress and this is a totally different one, in a different color," I said, fighting to get the hoop part that Frank had put in a separate hanging bag in the car.

"You won't be needing this," Frank said as he took the bag with the hoop in it away from me.

"No, Frank, I need it to hold the skirt out."

"No you won't. You'll see. Now go." And with that he leaned the hoop against the tree and gently kissed me on the cheek, moved me in behind the wheel, closed the door and waved goodbye. I could have sworn he was wiping a tear from his eye when I looked at him through the rear view mirror. I felt like crying myself since the day had come to put this monstrosity on and allow others to see me in it.

Y Y Y

THE LONG AWAITED wedding—by Angela, Angela's

mother and Nana only—was upon us. No long engagement for Angela when that gold American Express card was waiting for the shopping charges she was planning to rack up once she was Mrs. Angelo Tuddo.

Two hours before the rehearsal dinner all the bridesmaids arrived at Angela's house with our hair coiffed like we were going to wear it the day of the wedding—like that mattered if it was going to be under that enormous hat—with our dresses and matching dyed shoes. This morning, before going to Julia's I had a command performance at a nail salon where one of Angela's many aunts arranged for and treated all the bridesmaids to have manicures and pedicures together. It seemed to me this was the female version, Italian style, of a bachelor party. I expected the manicurist would be instructed to paint tiny flags of Italy in red, green and white on each nail but we were all given a French manicure and pedicure along with Angela. The Italian thing was not forgotten, however, because another aunt brought T-shirts custom made in red, green and white that said BRIDE of the FORTUNATA / TUDDO WEDDING and the date, while the rest of us got to wear the one that said BRIDESMAID of the FORTUNATA / TUDDO WEDDING. Angela's mother had one with MOTHER OF THE BRIDE and Mrs. Tuddo had the MOTHER OF THE GROOM with the mandatory addition of the FORTUNATA / TUDDO WEDDING, with the date. Nana had one too, without her nickname. Angela wanted all of us to wear our T-shirts to the rehearsal dinner. I advised I had come straight from the office and didn't have a change of clothes to wear with a T-shirt. She suggested I wear it like a muumuu over my business suit. This just kept getting better and better.

Angela had flower displays the size of bushel baskets delivered and waiting for us at her parents' home where the photo session for the bridesmaids was going to take place. There were so many people having to carry so much stuff we looked like nomads roaming the desert with all our possessions. Finally, after much hand wringing by Angela's mother in front of Angela's father, Mr. Donnato called and hired a limo bus to come and get all of our dresses, hoops, shoes, bushel baskets, and suitcases and bring it all to the hotel where we were staying the night of the church rehearsal and sit down dinner party to follow.

At Angela's parents' house a photographer was taking bridesmaids' photos ahead of time to minimize the photos needing to be taken at the church and reception. This was a good idea because he would need a bull horn and whip to corral some forty or so people in the wedding party. Doing that would be quite an accomplishment, since he also needed ten more hands for his camera, as well as the flash and the three video setups he was instructed to manage in order to capture the wedding every second, from every angle.

𝚼 𝚼 𝚼

AT ANGELA'S, I pulled the dress on to discover that Frank had replaced the hoop with yards and yards of netting to make the dress stand out away from me. It was softer and felt a lot more comfortable. The lines of the dress looked more natural than that hoop thing with the varying sized wires making everyone else look like a Christmas tree. He also cut the sleeves down so that the poofs didn't look like

Mount Fuji sitting on each shoulder. Now it was showing off the neckline and my cleavage more. To say it was pretty this way, or in any way was a bit of a stretch, but it did look better and it was a lot easier to move about in. I could actually sit down without pulling the hoop up to my waist and hoping my ass found a chair to land in. It also allowed me to stand next to someone and not hold them out at an arm's length. This didn't go unnoticed by the other bridesmaids.

"Why does your dress look...different...better?" asked bubble-gum-girl. The bridesmaid next to her had teased her hair so much her hat looked like it was an open sun umbrella on a pole. Bubble-gum-girl and high-hair-girl were giving me the once over, trying to figure out the difference in our dresses. I wore my hair in a simple braid down the back so if the hat came off, my hair wouldn't look like it had been molded into its shape. Their do was going to be interesting when they removed the hats.

"Maybe Angela wanted mine a little different since I'm the maid of honor?" I said and smiled. I stood behind other hoops and avoided any front row photos, hoping to remain unnoticed by Angela, her mother and the Scowler for as long as possible. I didn't want to be ordered to retrieve that hoop. Angela was self-absorbed with making the tiara fit perfectly on her head and didn't pay attention to the dress discussion. Angela's mother and Nana were all eyes on the sofa.

Angela's mother was standing by, wringing both hands as usual. She had been told by the photographer to remove the clear plastic covers on all her furniture, otherwise the flash would bounce off the plastic and explode light into the pictures causing overexposure or starbursts. This was probably the first time the furniture had ever been exposed to elements in the real world since it had arrived there some thirty years ago. She made a point of reminding all of us that the furniture was a wedding gift to her and Angela's father from Nana, who stood with hands clasped at her waist sending a disapproving look at us over Mrs. Fortunata's shoulder. Angela's mother, with the help of Nana, the Scowler, scanned the bridesmaids continuously looking for a drink or food in someone's hands that might spill onto the prized sofa and soil it. When Angela's mother was not commanded to stand in a photo she would pick up the plastic furniture covers, ready to replace them as soon as the last flash went off. As soon as the photographer said he was done, Angela's mother shooed everyone off the sofa and began to replace the plastic covers even while Angela whined to be unbuttoned.

🍸 🍸 🍸

WHEN THE PHOTOS were over I hurriedly changed so Angela, her mother and old eagle eye Nana didn't have a chance to look me over. Don't misunderstand, it was still an ugly dress, only a tad less ugly than what the others were wearing. Even with Frank's modifications, which I must say made the wearing of it much more tolerable, there was no way I would put this wicked thing on again…ever…to go anywhere…for any reason.

The buses hauled the entire wedding party to the church rehearsal then to the Court of Two Sisters in the French Quarter for the evening. Mr. Fortunato had booked rooms for the entire wedding party at the Hotel

Monteleone, walking distance from the restaurant, for the night. The buses would pick us up from the Monteleone and bring us to the church the next morning. Angela was getting married at a church on St. Charles Avenue reputed to have the longest aisle for brides to walk down in the City of New Orleans.

After the wedding ceremony, limos would pick us up from church and transport the happily married couple with their entourage to the Italian suburb of New Orleans—Metairie—and the Italian reception venue of choice—The Veranda. There was no mistaking The Veranda as Italian owned, operated and frequented because the semi circular drive was lined in an assortment of marble statues, all copies of great Italian sculptures. The oversized leaded, and bulletproof, glass doors opened to an entryway that looked over marble floors that zigzagged and changed configuration, color and design at every doorway for a dizzying effect if you looked down too long. Everything was exaggerated, oversized and overdone.

Their true claim to fame was the food the Veranda served at weddings—New Orleans style food, i.e. crab cakes, crab etouffee, oyster patties, and Italian food, i.e. Veal Parmesan, pastas and cannoli pastries. There was no end to the liquor served, all top shelf ending with Frangelico and Amaretto liquors. If it was Italian or made in Italy it was served here.

I asked Jiff to be my date to the wedding but I really couldn't imagine how it would help our relationship subjecting him to the rehearsal at the church and the dinner afterwards. Dante would be there and with so many people involved it would take hours to get them organized just to walk down the aisle and back. The church rehearsal had all the makings of a Chinese fire drill. Instead of joining me for the evening of Italian mayhem, Jiff was going to the church for the ceremony and then he'd meet me at The Veranda afterwards for the cocktail reception. Unlike wedding receptions elsewhere with sit down dinners, New Orleans wedding receptions are cocktail parties with endless trays of drinks, champagne and large appetizer portions served while everyone dances to live music. While the party was in full swing, after the wedding cake was cut and the bouquet and garter had been tossed, I was going to change out of the dress and Jiff and I planned to duck out to go somewhere else.

I assumed Dante would continue to avoid me as he'd been doing for the last several weeks, and we would only have to walk together down the aisle and out of the church to the waiting limos after the wedding. How hard could it be to be civil to one another? Besides, he was probably bringing Hanky Panky as his date. She should get a good laugh at my expense when she got an eyeful of me in this dress.

🍸 🍸 🍸

AT THE CHURCH, the rehearsal went way better than I ever could have imagined. The boatload of Italians remained quiet listened to the priest and followed his directions. The bridesmaids all marched up and down the aisle with military precision in the correct order and met our waiting groomsman, then stood exactly where we were told. When the priest indicated what he would say when the ceremony was over, we all turned in unison, met our escorts and proceeded down the aisle flawlessly. Even the young children, flower girls and ring bearers, listened and did their part without crying or throwing tantrums. The rehearsal moved as if pod people had taken the place of the entire wedding party with the exception of me. No one really had time to speak or stand next to each other very long. Dante and I avoided eye contact and he remained distant. It was just as well because the ordeal with Julia was putting a strain on me. The case against Julia was definitely in the police's favor and while I didn't want to be the one to spill a state secret I was hoping Dante might tell me something Julia could use.

As we exited the church Dante dropped my arm like it was on fire and the real members of the wedding party shed the pod people and returned to their normal, arm waving, screaming selves. Mr. Tuddo was waiting outside of church and instructed us all, over his bullhorn, to remain with our bridesmaid or groomsman, and sit together on the buses. It would make it easier to find our names on the placement cards when we arrived at the restaurant. He said we were all seated together in pairs. Dante and I would be joined at the hip all evening.

The bus ride wasn't bad since there were a lot of distractions. It seemed the bridesmaids could only communicate by yelling at each other in conversation and then letting out a long scream to indicate their side of the communication was over. They all talked—correction, screamed—at once to each other or their groomsman. Dante and I rode in silence, acting profoundly interested in everything being screamed around us rather than with each other.

There were two long parallel tables with the future bride, groom and their parents on the dais table across the end of both. And there they were, Brandy Alexander's name and Dante Deedler's name, side by side at the end of one table up against the dais. Dante was wedged between the head table and me. When we squeezed into the tightly configured seats, our thighs were touching. I didn't say a word except "excuse me" every time I bumped him with my elbow or foot. I never looked at him. I started to press my thigh into his a little more as the evening progressed and the wine flowed. I increased how many times I accidently bumped him with my elbow or foot. I could see it out of my peripheral vision that the vein on his neck was working overtime indicating he was at the boiling point but he refused to speak to me.

As soon as dinner was over, he excused himself and left. I stayed and chatted with a couple of people sitting near me, but when I saw Little Tony making his way in my direction, I decided it was time to go. During dinner I'd discovered we were paired or in foursomes to share rooms at the hotel. I was lucky enough to be roomies with two bridesmaids and Angela. Oh boy, a slumber party with a bunch of yats gossiping all night. Why couldn't any of these women have a conversation without screaming? My ears would be ringing for a week.

Angela's parents were in the adjoining room via a door they closed but did not lock so Angela could run back and forth between her friends and parents whining about every detail that might ruin her perfect day.

🍸 🍸 🍸

THE MORNING OF the wedding, when I woke up and opened my eyes I could have sworn the heavens parted and I heard the celestial "Ahhhhh" of angels singing. The bridesmaids were all abuzz getting dressed, doing their hair—more teasing—and trying to wrestle the hoops into place. Finally, someone knocked on our hotel room door and when it opened Little Tony stood there and advised all the bridesmaids it was almost time to get in the limos and head for the church. He said someone would come back for us in five minutes. The bridal party, Angela and her parents, all the flower girls and ring bearers would be leaving shortly. The girls began rushing about, frantically putting on last minute lipstick applications, looking for their hats, gathering the flower baskets and making final adjustments to the hoops.

When the second knock came and the door opened it was Dante, who held the door for us. I was the last one out and as I passed him he grabbed me around my waist and pulled me backwards into the room. He didn't say a word. He looked at me and nodded his head up and down asking for approval. I nodded yes. He held up one finger to his lips to indicate we needed to be quiet.

He removed my hat and threw it on the bed. I dropped the basket. He reached down and started at my feet gathering up yards of my dress and holding it up until he got both hands to my waist and then, pulling me into him, he reached around and put his hands on my rear. He lifted me up and I wrapped my legs around him. He walked me over to the door between the rooms. He leaned my back onto the closed adjoining door of the Fortunatas' room. I could hear the Fortunatas yelling at each other on the other side. Angela's mother was telling

Angela how beautiful she looked while Mr. Donnato was yelling he couldn't find his keys. Angela was screaming it was time to go. They were only a couple of feet away from us and the fact they could open the door any second and we could fall into their room bumped me to the top of my arousal meter. Once I had my legs around his waist and my arms around his neck, his hands were pulling off my panties and his mouth was all over my face. He pulled at my underwear and I pulled my legs up one at a time while one of his hands stayed on my rear and he could get them off with the other. I could not think of anything else but kissing him. When he got the panties off, he put me down. He put my panties in his tuxedo pocket and walked out the room.

I stood there breathless and leaning on the door until I could get steady on my feet. It took me a few minutes for me to compose myself. With trembling hands I put on fresh lipstick and sort of glided down the stairs on weak knees to meet the rest of the bridal party. I was so hot inside I thought people would step back from the heat that was radiating off me.

"Oh, good, here's Brandy, now we can all go." Mr. Donnato kissed me on the cheek, held the door open and helped me into the limo. I guess he had found his keys.

At the back of the church Little Tony was buzzing around any bridesmaid that would give him a cordial response. He was supposed to be escorting guests to their seats on the proper side of the church, either the groom's side or the bride's side. He was also supposed to walk Angela's mother to her seat so the wedding could commence. Most of us ignored him. I noticed bubble-gum-girl and another one of the Italian cousins with the high-hat-hair break away from our cluster and follow Little Tony into an alcove off the entry way. They were standing with their backs to me in a huddle blocked from the others by a curved wall. The church collection baskets were stored there out of sight. I moved a step away from the bridal party but stood close enough to look like I was still with the group. I could see Little Tony setting up lines of coke on the back of his hand and the three of them were snorting with a rolled up dollar bill.

Angela and her parents were going to wring Little Tony's neck if they caught him doing this in church while he was delegated as the family representative to be greeting and escorting guests. He was going to be high along with two of the bridal bimbos for the whole wedding. I moved back to the wedding party and took my place as maid of honor in front of Angela. Mr. Donnato was beaming and so proud to be escorting his daughter on her wedding day.

Finally, Angela's mother decided it was time to start the wedding and she needed to be seated, so she started the search for Little Tony. One of the bridesmaids not partaking in the pre-wedding snort pointed toward the alcove when Mr. Donnato starting asking where he was. Little Tony made a glassy eyed appearance to walk his mother to her seat. Mr. Donnato gave him a slap on the back of his head when Little Tony stood next to his parents. A church custodian opened the doors from the vestibule where we were waiting, revealing the six hundred or so guests turned in their seats and looking to the back where we all stood.

He straightened his tuxedo jacket by pulling it down from the bottom, held out his arm for his mother to take and then walked her up to her seat high fiving every guy he knew sitting on the aisle.

Mr. Donnato said, "I'm gonna kill that little bastard."

Angela started pleading, "Da-a-a-a-ddy, ple-e-e-e-ase, not toda-a-a-a-ay."

"OK, OK, don't worry baby, I'll kill him tomorrow." He hushed her. "You look beautiful, don't worry about your worthless brother right now."

Little Tony finally got his mother to her seat when trumpets blasted, indicating the wedding could commence. The trumpets were so loud they scared all the children in the wedding party, who started crying. When they saw all the guests turned in their seats looking back at them it sent them into a screaming frenzy. No one could coerce them into participating. The mothers of the flower girls carried crying babies up the aisle while they hid their faces on their mother's shoulders. The ring bearers had a similar experience except they shouted "NO" when their mothers tried to pick them up and walk with them. They threw themselves on the floor of the church screaming, and their fathers had to pick them up and move to a seat sending the rings up the aisle with an unemotional third party. The eighteen bridesmaids who had been bivouacking all around the back of the church migrated to their places in the lineup. The bridesmaids who had a nose full from Little Tony were acting bizarre, which came as no surprise to most of us. One all but jogged up the aisle and the other had to be pushed along by the bridesmaid behind her because she was walking so slowly she didn't seem to be moving at all. When she got to the front of the church she drifted behind the groomsman she met and stood next to him on the wrong side. One of the bridesmaids already in position had to move her to her proper spot, which wasn't easy, maneuvering around in the hoops.

When it was my turn to walk up the aisle, I saw my parents sitting on the aisle end of the pew so they had a good view of the procession and Jiff sitting, two pews behind them, also at the end of a row. He was looking at me coming up the center of church and smiling like he does whenever he sees me for the first time that day. That smile makes me feel like I've been scooped up in his arms and he is carrying me off into the sunset while I put my head on his shoulder. His smile and his look for me always melted my heart just like it was doing now.

In the same pew with Jiff was Julia, Frank and Woozie, all dolled up and looking spectacular. When I passed Jiff, he smiled at me and said "nice hat" just loud enough for me to hear when I looked at him. When I passed my parents, my dad mouthed, "smile" followed by a big toothy grin indicating I should do the same. My mother was in training to take over for The Scowler.

I looked up to the front of church just as the bridesmaid before me met her groomsman. They bowed their heads at the altar then parted to stand on either side of the altar. Dante stepped out to the middle of the aisle and turned so he was looking straight at me. I thought about where my underwear was and all of a sudden I could barely breathe. My head was thinking one thing and my heart was feeling another. I was so glad I didn't have to say anything for at least an hour until the ceremony was over. I wasn't sure what I was even going to say to Dante then.

It seemed the organist played for an eternity so that

eighteen bridesmaids could all walk up to the altar and get in position before another eardrum-piercing trumpet blast announced the bride's arrival.

The church ceremony, the music, the bride and groom were all a blur. The only thing clear to me was Dante waiting at the end of my long walk to the front of the church at the altar. He was watching me and when our eyes met, I felt weak in the knees with butterflies in my stomach. When I got to him I was almost breathless. He stepped forward, took my hand, squeezed it, we faced the altar together, then separated to stand in our appropriate spots on either side of Angela and Angelo. Those few seconds of him touching me sent my mind into a tailspin.

I couldn't stop thinking of his hands on me back in the hotel room and now my underwear was in his pocket. I was in church, for heaven's sake. I prayed to God no one needed to sneeze forcing Dante to reach for a handkerchief.

Catholic weddings are traditional with long-drawn-out ceremonies full of showing homage and asking for favors from the saints and patrons of families. But an Italian Catholic wedding was the all-out, hands-down, longest running ceremony with homages paid to every known saint, the bride's mother, and the groom's mother, in addition to an hour long mass. Each tribute required the bride to move around the church stopping at an altar or shrine, saying a prayer, lighting a candle or leaving a memento like a rose or flower. Her maid of honor (yes— me) goes with her, bending over in that dress and hat while holding a bushel basket to straighten the wedding gown behind her. Keeping the hat on my head while I bent over was a major accomplishment. I wanted to kiss Frank on the lips for removing the hoop, considering where my panties were, because every time I would have had to bend over in a hoop skirt I would have mooned everyone in the church. Finally, after the bride and groom thanked and prayed to every patron saint and statue in the church, it was time for Angela and Angelo to repeat their vows after the priest. Then, we all heard the long awaited, "You may now kiss the bride." After their wedding smooch, the priest announced, "Ladies and Gentlemen, Mr. and Mrs. Angelo Tuddo."

A trumpet blasted, again ringing in an encore of babies wailing while the church bells rang, birds sang—if only in my head—indicating the ceremony was over and it was time for the bride and groom to go forth and live happily ever after. Dante stepped up to take my arm and escorted me out of the church. As soon as he touched me I wanted to find an empty pew to make out in. He took my arm and pulled me tightly against him, which was possible given the alterations, Frank had made on the dress. *Where was that dang hoop when I needed it?*

Outside the church Dante wouldn't let go of my arm. We were the first couple out of the church right after the bride and groom. Before Jiff, Julia, Frank and Woozie could exit the church, Dante ushered me over to the waiting limo and pushed me inside. We were the only ones in it and he closed the door and hit the electronic lock while the entire wedding party was outside greeting and laughing with the invited guests exiting the church.

"I have something of yours," he said. Then his mouth was kissing my neck.

"We can't be doing this here," I attempted to say

through deep breaths while he moved his mouth from my neck, working down to my chest, kissing me. "This is making me nervous. I have Jiff meeting me."

"Do you want me to stop?" he asked, and started biting my ear.

My hormones answered him, "I want us to be anywhere but here, preferably somewhere we could take our clothes off."

A tapping on the tinted glass window indicated other people needed to get in the vehicle.

Once the door unlocked the flood of hats and tuxedos overwhelmed us. Since I was the one with the most maneuverability, I had to sit on Dante's lap to make room for the other bridesmaids and their hoop skirts. The hats were all pushing each other and they bent down around our heads like umbrellas. We were both hidden under mine and Dante had his hands all over me pulling me against him kissing my neck. I was on fire for Dante and wanted to be alone with him, not going to a party with six hundred people and where my date would be waiting for me.

Chapter Eighteen

THE BRIDAL PARTY spilled out of the limos at the reception hall and I spotted Julia, Frank and Woozie among the guests talking with Jiff before we were ushered upstairs to a second floor private bridal room of The Veranda. Here, the photographer could take photos while the entire wedding party was in one place before we scattered all over the reception like bugs when you turn on a light. The Tuddos, Angelo the groom and his father, who looked like three hundred pound bookends, were in no way walking up the curving stairwell to the second floor. Instead they got onto motorized scooters waiting at the door for them to ride around the reception. Due to their combined weight—a few cannoli over the freight elevator's limit—they had to take turns in the lift to the second floor where they exited right next to the catering stairs used for the kitchen staff to bring up food and drinks. They scooted out the elevator, grabbed a drink and made their way into the room with the rest of us. This exclusive area on the second floor was off limits to the rest of the guests with its own powder rooms and bathrooms for the bridal party to freshen up and relax for a few minutes without waiting in the lines for rest rooms or food service downstairs. The powder rooms were oversized, filled with sofas and settees to accommodate trying to sit in any and all dresses they have probably seen over the years. The ladies could sit a few minutes, freshen up for the photos or rest their feet from tight shoes.

After all of the women made their initial ladies' room stop we were commanded to pose in several group shots of the entire wedding party. This was the first time we had all been in one place in our wedding attire. One entire wall of the private salon was painted with a southern columned mansion like Tara, the plantation home in *Gone With The Wind*. After trying every conceivable configuration to get all eighteen bridesmaids and seventeen hoops in one photo, the photographer said some of the bridesmaids had to remove the hoops and stand behind the dresses with hoops in the front row so we all could get in the picture. The otherwise happy going, smiling Mr. Fortunato went into a rage over the fact he spent all this money on this particular photographer who should have a wide-angle lens. The photographer, also Italian, began waving his arms around as much as Mr. Fortunato and screamed Rome didn't have this many Italians in one place when they elected a new Pope. He went on to say he had the largest wide-angle lens sold on planet earth and he still couldn't get us all in without doing a panorama shot. For that, we all had to remain absolutely still, no breathing; no blinking and he could not believe that was ever going to happen. He looked at bubble-gum-girl popping one when he yelled this. The hoops had to go.

Little Tony went to work offering his assistance to any woman who needed help with her hoop removal. When he got close to me, Dante stepped in front of him and he slithered off to annoy someone else.

The bridesmaids who had purses could leave them in this room since it was only open to the bridal party. I had stuffed my small purse in the bushel basket of flowers and decided to leave it in the room to pick up when I was ready to leave. I brought my lipstick, mirror, cell phone, house key and driver's license. I folded a twenty-dollar bill around my driver's license and house key and put it down the front of my dress. The rest I'd take my chances on being here when I was ready to leave.

After all the repositioning for the bridal party photos, a wait staff arrived via the back stairwell from the kitchen with food and champagne to toast the bride and groom. When the photographer was finished Mr. Fortunato was smiling and slapping him on the back like the good buddies they always were before the wide-angle lens, screaming match.

Dante did not move from my side. He got me another glass of champagne for the toast to the bride and groom after he took the one Little Tony had given me and put the empty glass on a tray after pouring it into a plant.

"What's wrong with you?" I asked through clenched teeth with a big fake smile on my face. "This is his sister's wedding. Little Tony is just trying to be nice."

"Let him be nice to one of the other seventeen girls here," Dante said and clinked his glass to mine. "Stay away from him."

"Please stop this. You're acting like you have me in protective custody." I took my champagne glass and tried to step away from him. He was starting to make me extremely nervous, standing close to me and acting like my personal bodyguard. This would have to stop by the time we got downstairs with the rest of the guests, where my parents and my date were waiting for me.

With the photographs done, the wedding party start-

ed downstairs for the mandatory Bride/Groom and
Father/Daughter dances and so the newly married couple
could greet and welcome their invited guests. Angela's
mother and father were all smiles and led the way. Angela
hopped on the back of the groom's scooter and rode
around the reception with him much like she was on the
back of a motorcycle with her wedding gown hiked up
around her. Mr. Tuddo was scooting around the
reception helping himself to anything on a tray that was
in arm's reach. Mrs. Tuddo—all ninety-eight nervous
pounds of her—tried to run interference with the cannoli
trays but she was obviously losing a lifetime battle in that
war. The bridesmaids, while happy to rid themselves of
the hats and baskets, struggled getting down the stairs in
hoops. They were advised by Angela's mother in English
and by Nana, the Scowler, in Italian, that they could not,
would not, take off the hoops until Angela and Angelo
left for their honeymoon later in the night. I saw Little
Tony hanging to the back of the room with some of his
gal pals. I'm sure they planned to snort up another line or
two before joining everyone on the dance floor.

Downstairs the Levee Men were already onstage and
played for the bridal party to dance. This was the only
time that the groom and his father left the scooters the
entire evening. Angela and her father danced, then the
other obligatory couples, Angela's mother and the groom,
the bride and groom and then entire wedding party
followed suit. Dante grabbed my arm taking me to the
dance floor just as I spotted Jiff talking with my dad at the
bar. I could imagine the conversation my father was into.
He was holding up a wine bottle and giving Jiff all the
details of how great he thought it was to have a vineyard

with your own wine named after you. Jiff's family could buy a vineyard if they wanted their name on a wine label.

Dante whirled me around the dance floor leading me in classic spins and turns to a waltz.

"Where did you learn to dance like this?" I asked. "I've never danced with you where you lead. I always lead. This feels weird, but nice. I like it."

"I've been taking lessons for this big event just to dance with you," he said, twirling and spinning me through dance moves with ease and confidence across the floor.

"Dance lessons? Where did you take dance lessons?" While I waited for his answer, I wondered if I was the only person here whose body had not been taken over by the pod people again? Everyone was acting the opposite of how they normally acted.

"My partner, Hanky, is a ballroom dance instructor. She's been teaching me." He led me through a double spin and back into his arms. "We're not…weren't… dating."

"Aww. I bet you want me to feel bad for not liking Hanky now, don't you?" I said. I put a finger to my lips and looked up toward the ceiling before I added, "Wait, let me think…I don't feel bad and I still don't like her."

"Look, I know you're here with that guy, but I'm taking you home tonight…don't argue. I still have something that belongs to you." The music stopped and Dante put his hand into his pocket. Jiff appeared and was standing next to us.

"Detective, nice to see you outside of our usual meetings. Please call me Jiff." Jiff held out his hand for Dante to shake.

Dante hesitated not taking his hand out of his pocket while I held my breath. I thought he was going to hand my underwear to Jiff or worse, do a second line around the floor with his new found dancing talent waving my underwear in the air over his head for all to see. After a long, awkward moment Dante shook Jiff's hand leaving the spoils of our earlier encounter hidden in his pocket.

"You can call me Detective Deedler." He said to Jiff, nodded to me then walked off toward the bar.

Jiff and I exchanged startled looks while I exhaled the breath I had been holding. I thought this was odd even for Dante. "Sorry for his behavior, but I'm not my brother's keeper," I said.

"I don't think he wants to be your brother," Jiff said. Then he waved his hand dismissing the Dante thing and looking me over said, "On you that dress looks…"

"Like the Superdome… a Mardi Gras float?" I cut him off with a big smile.

"Different on you… better than the others. What did you do to it?" he said taking it all in as he looked me up and down, holding my hand and twirling me. When I faced him again he pulled me into him and kissed my forehead saying, "You're the most beautiful Mardi Gras float in the room."

"Frank customized it for me and got rid of that miserable hoop the others are still wearing." I looked around at the bridesmaids dancing at arm's length while their dates were trying to lean in over the hoop. I was still in his arms so I looked up at him and said, "It looks like you met my dad."

"Yes, he said he recognized me from the parade. I didn't think anyone noticed that kiss between you and me, but your dad told me otherwise. In fact, he also told me Dante was standing right next to us working a detail that night. Why didn't you tell me that?"

I shrugged.

"He's a nice guy, your dad, and he really likes the wine being served," Jiff said.

"Yes. Chianti. Who knew? He's usually a Jameson's man, Irish, you know? Have you met my mother?" I asked hoping that awful social requirement was behind me and added a note to self to talk to my dad later about sharing information.

"No, not yet."

"Well, she's German like you, but don't expect that to carry any weight with her. She's equally indifferent to everyone, my date, Dante, German, Irish, Italian, it doesn't matter. I'm just warning you. Please don't take offense."

"I'll be on my best behavior. She might like me. Would you like me to get you a glass of wine or champagne?" We walked toward the bar where my dad was standing talking with Woozie. Jiff ordered a glass of champagne for me, and Chianti for himself. The bartender poured each drink into a 12 oz. white stadium cup commonly thrown in Mardi Gras parades. This one had the couples' black and white photo along with the date to commemorate this happy day. "Oh, they are serving red wine and champagne in white wedding go cups. How unusual," Jiff said studying the cups from every angle and top to bottom.

I knew it would be a mistake to expose him to this mega Italian throw down where the norm in this world was Chianti in a go cup while in Jiff's world it would be

Dom Perignon in crystal flutes.

We turned to leave the bar and stepped over to where my parents and Woozie were standing.

My mother, with her stellar ability to make everyone feel uncomfortable in her presence, totally ignored Jiff when I introduced him and cut me off asking, "Have you seen your sister?"

"I just seen Sherry. She went outside with one of them Deedler twins…to smoke," Woozie answered her.

"Smoke?" She made a beeline for the exit leaving the three of us to chat.

"Sherry's right over there," my dad said, nodding his head in her direction and smiling. Woozie acted like she didn't hear him.

"Really? Maybe it was someone else with one of the twins," I said. If Woozie had my back, I had hers.

My dad launched into questions, asking Woozie when was she coming back to their house to work when the music started up again and it was loud. Woozie was pointing to her ears and shaking her head like she couldn't hear him. Why couldn't it have started up two minutes ago so I could have avoided my mother? We put our glasses—correction—go cups down on a table and went to dance.

We caught the band's attention and waved hello to Maurice and the other members we knew. Julia and Frank were dancing and walked up to talk to us when the song finished.

"Julia, go stand somewhere else in that dress. You're making me look worse," I said to her. Frank had on the seersucker suit he said he would wear with a bowtie and was carrying a small clutch. It might have been Julia's but

I was afraid to ask.

"You know, there's a guy here I swear I've seen before," Julia said. "I just can't place him. He's short."

"Where is he? Point him out," I answered. "Is this someone you might want to dance with?"

"No, he's about five feet tall, and kinda greasy looking. I haven't seen him since y'all arrived. He's in the wedding party. I saw him when you all came in and went upstairs. I just feel like I know him from somewhere," she said.

"You must mean Little Tony. He's the bride's brother." I couldn't imagine from where or why Julia would know Little Tony. "He's a goof, avoid him like the plague."

Dante appeared and asked for the next dance. Jiff looked annoyed but being the gentleman he was he said, "Sure. I'll go say hi to Maurice," and excused himself. Julia and Frank went to dance but not before I saw the big eye roll she directed at me.

I kept a smile on my face, but through clenched teeth I asked, "What are you doing? I have a date and you're being rude to him and making me uncomfortable." I was starting to get good at talking while smiling. "Stop this."

"Do not leave here tonight unless you are with me, do you understand?" Dante said in my ear while we slow danced and he held me so tightly I could barely breathe. My desire for Dante was being replaced by a nervous meltdown. I couldn't see how this was going to work with the two of them here when it was time for me to leave with one of them.

In an attempt to get Dante out of there, I made up a little white lie. "I heard there's been a murder way out on

Chef Highway, almost to Mississippi. Don't you have to leave immediately to go and investigate?" I asked him.

"Nice try, but I'm off tonight. Hey, did you see the custom cups with the bride and groom's photo they made for their wedding?" Dante asked. "That's a cool idea."

I watched Jiff over Dante's shoulder every time I was facing his direction. Jiff was talking to Maurice, who came off the stage while the band played the melody. He was facing the dance floor in our direction and watching me dance with Dante while he spoke to Maurice. Their body language was tense and suggested it was more than a howdy talk. Maurice looked around the reception and pulled out his cell phone. He was showing Jiff something on it. Jiff looked up and scanned the room until he got Julia's attention and then waved her over.

"You know I have a date and he's taking me home?" I said to Dante. I was using what Woozie called the smart aleck attitude. "Do you want to join us?"

"Yes. That will work, because there is something I want to discuss with the both of you."

I was horrified and couldn't even keep up the pretense of smiling while talking. "What do you want to discuss with the two of us?" I couldn't imagine what he might have in mind since my underwear was still in his pocket. "I don't know why you waited until now to make your big move, if that's what this is. Is this supposed to make me realize how much you want me back? So, you do to it in front of Jiff? You are making me extremely uncomfortable."

I tried to reach in his pocket to retrieve my property discreetly, but Dante put his hand on mine before I could take them and said, "No way. I plan on putting these back where I found them."

The song ended and Dante led me by my hand over to where my parents were chatting it up with his. My mother was scoping out the room looking for my sister and the twins. My dad had a bottle of wine and was giving Mr. Deedler the briefing on the Fortunato vineyard in Italy. I'd heard it a too many times by now. Dante took an immediate interest in the wine bottle and let go of my hand. It was my chance to get away from him and back to Jiff. *What is it that had men so impressed with the wine thing*, I wondered.

As soon as I was free from Dante's clutches, Miss Ruth, Dante's mother, sprang into action and grabbed me in a bear hug saying how beautiful I looked, how much she missed me living next door and how perfect Dante and I looked just now dancing together. Then she started crying. I was being enveloped in Miss Ruth's big arms and big bosom with my face crushed into her shoulder. All that was not smothered in the hug were my eyes looking over her shoulder at my dad who was doing a big eye roll. We exchanged a quick look while I was still crushed in the hug. Miss Ruth had quite a grip, given the years she spent wrestling things away from her five boys she didn't want them to play with. I could see that Dante got the not wanting to let go part from his mother. Our dads were both 'go with the flow' kinda guys.

As soon as I could pull free I excused myself to go find my date. Dante didn't break from the wine bottle discussion but had a severe look on his face while the vein in his neck started to pump. Odd, I thought, over wine.

After the full court press from Miss Ruth, I needed a few quiet moments upstairs in the private bridal party room to fix my hair and freshen up. I'm sure I had her lipstick kiss still on my cheek. I needed a minute to decide how to handle Dante's weird behavior and how to leave with only one man. I was hoping I could get Julia to distract Dante while I left with Jiff. I didn't want a scene.

As I walked up the steps, I looked over my shoulder and saw Dante, Jiff and Julia conferring over Jiff's cell phone. I needed to take a few minutes by myself. I wanted this wedding over and my life back to normal, even if normal meant I'd be worrying about Julia and her murder investigation. At least, Dante and Jiff would not be in the same room.

When I came out of the powder room up in the bridal room, Little Tony was sitting at a table.

"I came up here to find you," he said.

"Well, I've been downstairs dancing this entire time. I can see why you missed me since the wedding party is so large," I said.

"We haven't had a drink or a dance all night." Little Tony's eyes had that drug glazed over look compared to his usual darting eye movements.

"Sure. Let's go downstairs and dance now." I tried to walk toward the reception room stairway. He grabbed me by my arm and swung me around away from the stairs and pushed me toward one of the small bistro tables.

"No, let's have a drink up here. Sit down." He picked up a wine glass from a set up on a nearby table and pulled a flask from his pocket. He poured red wine from the flask into the glass.

"Oh, is this your family's wine?" I asked him. "You know my dad really likes that stuff."

"Yeah, this is it. Drink up." He pushed the glass into

my hand.

I didn't like the way he was acting but I figured he was under the influence of God knows what by now making him more obnoxious than usual. I decided to sit and have a couple of sips then excuse myself saying I had to get back to my date.

"I'm more of a champagne drinker but this is really good wine. I see why my dad likes it," I said. I took another sip and set the wine glass down on the table. Little Tony picked up the glass and handed it back to me. "This is a great wedding and Angela made a beautiful bride, don't you think?"

"Yeah, Angela finally got what she wanted," he said.

"What about you? Any wedding bells in your future?" I asked him trying to steer him away from the wine. I really didn't care for Chianti.

"No. Why make one woman miserable when I can make them all happy?" he said, laughing at his own joke.

"Aren't you drinking with me?" I asked, taking another small sip and setting the glass down on the edge of the table so I could fumble around in my basket for my purse and cell phone. Making small talk with Little Tony was starting to become a chore.

"I can drink this stuff anytime I want too," he said. "I think you need to drink your wine so you don't hurt our feelings." Little Tony had a menacing look on his face.

"Yes, I'll have a little more. You know I'd never do anything to insult your family, Tony. I've known you and Angela since grade school." I looked into my purse and saw I had a missed call and text from Jiff on my cell.

Then I looked closer at the message from Jiff. "You mind? I have a message and I'm guessing it's from my date wondering where I am." As I removed my cell phone from my bag and read the screen, *Maurice says Little Tony is the guy who was following V.* Little Tony knocked the phone out of my hand and it went shooting across the floor.

"You're not talking with nobody," he said.

"What are you doing?" I asked. "If you broke my phone, you will be buying me a new one. What is wrong with you?"

"Finish your wine," he said.

Tony's actions sent a cold shiver down my spine. I started to feel a little dizzy from the wine at the same time. Jiff was trying to text me it was Little Tony who followed Violet around and probably supplied her with the drugs. He knew the band and he knew Maurice could identify him as having been seen with Violet. I was glad I was sitting down when I had this realization or I might have hit the floor on weak knees. He fit the description of the sleazy guy everyone said had been giving Violet the roofies. Why didn't I see it before now? How much of the wine did I drink? I wondered if it was enough to render me helpless.

"Drink your wine," he said again, "and then we're gonna go for a little ride. We're going out the back elevator, you and me." He grabbed my arm.

"Look Tony, you don't have to be so rough. Let's go downstairs and join the party, we'll dance…but I can't go for a ride. My date is downstairs waiting on me. He'll be up here looking for me any minute." I fought to keep my voice steady.

"Yeah, right."

I tried to get up again, and he slapped my face and

pushed me back in the chair. I rubbed my face where it stung and I picked up the glass as if to take another sip of the wine.

"You had to stick your nose where it didn't belong. You had to keep snooping with your attorney boyfriend downstairs about St. Germain and give your dad a bottle of our wine. You had to make sure everyone saw it." He pulled a gun out of his jacket and aimed it at me.

"Put that gun away, what's wrong with you? This is your sister's wedding. Your father, your father...he's going to be really ticked off at you if he finds out you have a gun here and you're aiming it at people." I thought I might be slurring my words because I really had to concentrate to speak. I looked to the stairway entrance to see if anyone was coming up who could help me.

"He ain't finding out. You ain't telling him cuz we gonna be long gone in a few minutes. Now you are gonna finish your wine and take a little ride with me. When I get back, the party will still be going and no one is gonna miss you. You think you're too good for me.... well after we get to know each other a little better I'm gonna make sure you never open that big mouth of yours again." He stepped in closer pushing the gun into my chest. It was one of those small, silver Saturday night specials that if you were shot with it, it wouldn't kill you but it could tear up your insides bouncing all over the place. This was what I recalled from Dante's Gun Lesson 101.

"Tony, anyone can walk in here right now. My parents and my date are waiting for me downstairs. Did you forget Dante's here?" I was feeling the effect of the drug from just a couple of sips. I really had to focus on the wine glass and act like I was going to pick it up. I wanted to throw it on Little Tony but I was having trouble making myself do what I was thinking about. I wasn't sure I could throw it let alone hit him.

"Dante don't know nothing and he won't come looking for you until that boyfriend of yours figures out you're missing. Maybe he'll think you left with Dante and Dante will think you left with him. Either way, I have plenty of time to get you outta here," he said pushing his face into mine.

Instead of drinking from the glass I dropped it. Everything looked like it was moving in slow motion. The glass shattered on the floor; Little Tony jumped back to avoid the spill and held his arms out in an effort not to get wine on his suit. I lunged toward the stairway leading downstairs and screamed. I couldn't tell if the music was playing too loud for anyone to hear me.

Then I was on the floor and Little Tony was trying to get me to my feet. He held the gun in one hand while dragging me with his other hand away from the stairway. When he couldn't get me to stand, he pulled me by the arm across the floor toward the freight elevator. If he got me into the freight elevator that opened out onto the loading dock, no one would see us leave. I tried screaming again. Maybe there was someone in the kitchen who might hear me down the back stairway.

The freight elevator opened and Dante was standing in it. Little Tony aimed the gun at him while still holding my arm he was dragging me by.

"You really want to shoot a cop?" Dante asked him. He was standing perfectly still with his arms to his side, no weapon drawn and he sounded very calm.

Little Tony looked like he might be trying to decide if

that was a good idea or not when I bit him on the leg. He jumped and looked down at me pointing the gun at me. Dante body slammed into him and they both slid across the floor with Dante on top. When they came to a stop, Little Tony tried to wrestle Dante off but Dante outweighed him by a lot. He knocked the gun out of Little Tony's hand, lifted him off the floor then cold cocked him. Tony hit the floor like a rag doll.

Dante called toward the kitchen back stairs and two uniform police came into the room with their guns drawn. They took over hauling Little Tony away. Dante knelt down and asked me if I was hurt. I shook my head no, but I was drowsy from the drug and just wanted to close my eyes.

The last thing I remember was Dante picking me up in his arms and carrying me down the back catering stairs. I put my head on his shoulder and passed out.

🍸 🍸 🍸

I WOKE UP and found myself in a very uncomfortable bed that looked like it was in a hospital room in a prison. The windows were all barred and there was a set of handcuffs dangling off the headboard above my head. Dante and Jiff were standing on either side of me. After looking back and forth from one to the other I said, "If I didn't already have this killer headache, seeing you two like this would definitely give me one. Where am I and how long have I been here?"

"We're at the police station," Jiff said. "We've been here about two hours. I don't think you ingested that much. I wanted to take you to a hospital." He looked at

Dante.

"How do you feel?" Dante asked me. He shot a look at Jiff and added, "I had the coroner come in and take a look at you. He said you'd be all right."

"The coroner said I'd be all right? Well, that's reassuring. Am I in the morgue?"

"No, you're in a medical room used by the police medical staff," Dante answered.

I sat up and then tried to get off the bed. "I'm OK, I think, just a little shaky. Little Tony, right?" I said.

"Yes." Dante said. He helped me stand and inspected me up and down to make sure I could stay up on my own. Then he continued, "We had a partial print from the wine bottle found in the dumpster but his prints weren't in the system. The back label on the wine bottle was destroyed and illegible when forensics got it so all we had to go on was the front label. It only had the wine's name on it, none of the information on the vineyard or where it came from. When your dad showed it to me tonight I realized how it all connected. We had Little Tony in our sights for a while waiting to make an arrest on drug charges. We had him figured for roofies and cocaine. We just couldn't tie him to Violet and St. Germain."

"When you were dancing, Maurice showed me a photo he took when y'all came in from the limos," Jiff said. "He took one of Little Tony because he recognized him as the guy who followed Violet around. I asked Julia to look at it and she remembered seeing him at Pancake Paddy's when she went there for coffee. I sent it to Ernest and got him to go there and verify it with the manager."

"Jiff came over and told me when I was looking at the

label your dad was showing me. We both saw you go upstairs," Dante said while Jiff nodded his head.

"Oh, my God, I think Little Tony has been following me," I sat back down. "The wine he gave me had Rohypnol in it. He tried to force me to drink all of it."

"I sent it to the lab for evidence," Dante said. "I don't need it tested to know it's going to be a match."

"You could have been shot coming in there like that," I said.

"No, I wasn't going to let him kill me because I still have unfinished business with you." He looked right at Jiff when he said it. He looked back at me and said, "Little Tony had been drinking and he was also high so I knew his reaction time was going to be off. Besides, shooting a cop is big a deal, even to a loser like him. They all figure they will get away with shooting someone but the whole police force comes after you when you shoot a cop. Even the worse criminals think twice," Dante said.

"He said he was going to get to know me better before he killed me," I said.

"That little weirdo has been a freakazoid since we were kids. He thinks he's a tough guy? Well, I'm going to make him sorry he ever even said that to you." Dante's vein was starting to pump and I grabbed his hand.

"Thank you for saving me. It's hard to imagine someone I've known since we were kids could be such a, such a…" I said.

"Psycho," Jiff finished. "You hit call back when you picked up your phone. I'm guessing it was right before Little Tony knocked it away from you, so when I heard what was going on, I hit record. We have everything he said to you recorded. You got him."

"So, the three of us all left together?" I asked rubbing my temples with my fingers.

Dante reached over and extended his hand to Jiff and said, "Thanks for your help."

Jiff said, "I'll go get the car and meet you out front. Dante, can you walk her out?"

"Of course." Hanky appeared in the doorway and Dante told her he'd be with her in a minute.

"She's a good dance instructor," I said, "but I still don't like her."

"She took Jiff's statement while I waited here with you. Jiff gave us the recording. Little Tony is toast. Hanky will wait and take Maurice's statement and any of the band members after they finish playing tonight. I told them I didn't want to make a scene at the wedding for Angela or her parents. After Jiff showed me the cell photo Maurice took of Little Tony and said he's the one who followed St. Germain and Violet around, we saw you going upstairs alone and I realized I hadn't seen Little Tony since we got to the reception. I figured he might still be up here waiting on you. He's good at waiting."

Dante told me he carried me down the back stairway and had the uniformed police haul Little Tony discreetly down the same way through the kitchen. Jiff met us in the back of the building and took us to the police station in his Mercedes. We left unnoticed and without making a scene except to the kitchen staff.

"C'mon," Dante said. "Jiff needs to take you home."

Dante walked me out to Jiff's car. As it pulled up he said, "I'll be awhile. Will you wait up for me?"

I'm just a sucker for a man in a tuxedo with a loosened bow tie at his neck. Dante looked handsome in the tuxedo he was wearing in spite of it being rumpled a bit with a dusty mark on the pants where he had slid across the floor with Little Tony. His jacket had a ripped pocket so he wasn't going to get his deposit back.

"I'll be up," I said.

He took my hand and kissed it walking away from me backwards and then he left to finish his paperwork and book Little Tony as Jiff got out his car and came around to open my door.

Y Y Y

AT MY FRONT door Jiff hugged me and said he was so glad I wasn't hurt. He said he was sorry he wasn't more help to me. I told him, I was sorry *I* wasn't more help to me. I told him it took a few minutes before I realized Little Tony was the bad guy and he was going to hurt me. I had a couple of sips of the wine before I realized it had the drug in it.

Jiff said Dante told him the police had held out releasing what the wine label looked like because they couldn't find anyone who imported it. They wanted to question the importer but were running into dead ends. The wine bottle from the dumpster did have Rohypnol traces, the same chemical makeup as what was found in St. Germain and Julia's tox screens. The police were convinced it was the bottle from the room and the one that drugged Julia and St. Germain. Dante told Jiff he never thought Julia was guilty even though so much pointed in her direction. Dante thought once they could tie the wine bottle to someone they would have the killer and they did.

"We both have had a long day, especially you. Dante is going to recommend dropping all charges against Julia," Jiff said.

"Don't you mean Detective Deedler when you are referring to Dante?" I joked.

"He said I could call him Dante at the police station. I'm surprised you didn't hear that? He actually thanked me for my help with the photo."

"Really?" I must have been more drugged than I thought. "Can we talk tomorrow? I'm really tired," I said.

Jiff hugged me, kissed my forehead and said, "We've both had a long, stressful night." Then his voice got a little shaky and he hugged me tighter saying, "I don't know what I would have done if something had happened to you…if you had been hurt. I'll call you tomorrow." Then he left me alone wanting a whole lot more physical comfort.

It was an hour later when Dante called. He told me over the phone Little Tony confessed he had given Violet the wine spiked with Rohypnol to finally put the moves on her. When he went to her place that night to open the bottle she told him she had given it to Gervais St. Germain because that afternoon Gervais had told her he loved her. Violet was angry with St. Germain once she realized he wasn't going to celebrate his profession of love with her so she followed him when he left her. She discovered he was staying in a hotel and saw him go out with Julia. Trouble follows trouble and Little Tony followed Violet. When he found where Gervais was staying he wanted that wine back before he was implicated in Gervais drugging someone and it all came back on him since the family name was plastered all over the bottle. Little Tony followed Violet, Julia and St. Germain back to the hotel after watching them at the Napoleon House. We know Violet went to meet the friend at a bar to drink and was there when the murder took place. Little Tony knew who Julia was from hanging out at Pancake Paddy. He climbed the tree to get a better look and saw a way to gain entry so he waited to make his move. When he saw them drinking the wine he knew it was just a matter of time before they passed out. This was his opportunity to get rid of his nemesis, have Violet to himself and frame someone else for killing Gervais. He picked up Julia's dress, covered the statue in it and bashed in St. Germain's head. He said he rinsed out the glasses thinking he eliminated the drug and took the wine bottle. He said he left the hotel about 1:45 am and went looking for Violet. The time he left the hotel tracks with the coroner's time of death. His mistake was to dump the items together so close to the hotel. He figured the police would find the dress and statue and tie them to Julia without looking any further. When Julia's attorney proclaimed there was a missing wine bottle possibly laced with Rohypnol, the police looked closer at the one found in the dumpster with the dress and statue.

Tony spilled it all thinking he might get himself a lighter sentence. He told Dante he got antsy and started following me to see if I could tie him to the murder. He worried I might remember seeing that wine bottle at my Dad's house the night they were there announcing Angela's upcoming marriage.

"You know if you talk to someone five minutes you will know someone they know or grew up with here in New Orleans. Imagine what you'll find out if you sit and watch them everyday," Dante said.

"Really. And here's Julia thinking she didn't know anyone other than St. Germain and she'd seen both Violet and Little Tony at the coffee house," I said.

"I'm leaving the station now. I know it's late, but I have something of yours that I'd like to return personally."

"I'm still up," I said. "I'll put on a pot of coffee."

The End

Watch for more with Brandy Alexander in…

Drive-Thru Murder
Book 3 of the New Orleans Go Cup Chronicles

About the Author

Colleen Mooney has owned and driven motorcycles, raced her sailboat on Lake Pontchartrain and in long distance competition across the Gulf of Mexico, crewed on super yachts racing in Key West and has been scuba diving from Florida's panhandle to the Maldives. Her love of snow skiing has taken her to slopes from New York to Colorado and the Alps. She loves to relive and write about these adventures, the people she meets and her beloved hometown of New Orleans.

Her first career was 20+ years in sales and marketing with AT&T. Colleen has lived in Birmingham, AL, Morristown, NJ, New York City and Atlanta, GA. Her second career is in real estate but she will tell you the work that makes her heart sing is animal rescue. Schnauzer Rescue of Louisiana is a breed rescue Colleen directs. Her love of dogs and her keen observations of her fellow New Orleanians and their antics inspired her to write her first book, 'Rescued By A Kiss.' (2014)

When Colleen isn't writing, diving or picking up abandoned dogs, she likes to spend time with friends and family enjoying favorite local restaurants and food.

You can take the girl out of New Orleans, but you can't take the New Orleans out of the girl!

You can contact Colleen at colleen@colleenmooney.com, or visit her online to stay informed on upcoming books, contests or just see what Colleen is up to with the following:

Website:

www.colleenmooney.com

Facebook:

facebook.com/ColleenMooneyAuthor

Twitter:

twitter.com/mooney_colleen

OR

To find out more about Schnauzer Rescue visit their webpage, Facebook or email and share photos of your BFF with us here:

www.nolaschnauzer.com
facebook.com/nolaschnauzer
Email: nolaschnauzer@gmail.com

Made in the USA
Columbia, SC
21 July 2019